Goes to London

EAGLE ASHCROFT

Wasteland Press
Shelbyville, KY USA
www.wastelandpress.net

Nibs Goes To London
by Eagle Ashcroft

First Printing - January 2007
ISBN13: 978-1-60047-075-2
ISBN10: 1-60047-075-0

Printed in the U.S.A.

Dedicated to Helen M. Bezansky & Joyce Carter, my sister

WATCH FOR THESE OTHER NIBS MISADVENTURE STORIES:

Niles

Goes to London

FORWARD

Nibs is a fourteen year old black and white half Persian tom cat who can speak through his elderly owner who lives in a run down cockroach infested tenement building on social security. One of his master's cousins dies and leaves Nibs an estate worth three hundred billion dollars. Nibs hires on some servants, buys a yacht and goes off to London where their customs get him and his servants in trouble and they are thrown in jail. The action is a hilarious non-stop adventure that will have you laughing so hard that tears will come to your eyes and you may roll out of your chair. This is the first in a series of twenty six short stories in several volumes of the misadventures of Nibs.

CHAPTER ONE

THE INHERITANCE

Mr. Cuttleworth is an elderly man in his late sixties who wears large lenses glasses and is slightly stooped, wears old fashion style tattered suits, is bare-headed and has gray hair. Nibs is a long-haired black and white half Persian tom cat and is fourteen years old, but still very active.

Mr. Cuttleworth and his cat Nibs are sitting on a thread bare couch in a dingy run down cockroach infested small living room of an old tenement building in Pleasant Grove, Indiana. There are old newspapers and out dated magazines piled atop his couch, on an old coffee table, shelves and about the floor. An over stuffed faded armchair sets across from the couch. An old torn pull down shade half covers the single old window overlooking a dirty litter covered vacant long one story below. The walls have well worn old style pink flowered wallpaper. A few old water stained prints in their cheap frames hang at lope sided angles on the walls. An old ceramic lamp with faded yellow shade is the only light in the room. It sets on a rickety end table. A bald worn hardwood door is on the wall leading in to the hall. There is an open doorway in to a cluttered kitchen at another end of the room. Mr. Cuttleworth is reading an old yellow colored newspaper.

"You know Nibs; it seems the world is getting worse every day. Why it says right here in the newspaper that President Roosevelt is going to run for a third term. What does he want to be, a lifetime president? He ought to quit while he is ahead and give someone else a chance at it. What's that you say Nibs? Oh you're right as usual I'm reading an old out of date paper. But that's not the point Nibs, the point is a president should never try hogging all leadership of a country and…"

Just then a knocking can be heard at the door. Mr. Cuttleworth puts down his paper and turning his head looks toward the door as he asks "Who is it?"

A women's voice is heard coming from the other side of the door: "Mr. Cuttleworth! This is Mrs. Burnside, your landlady! I need to talk to you about your rent!"

"Alright just a minute, I'll have to get up and come unlock the door I'll be there in just a minute."

Mr. Cuttleworth slowly gets up from the old couch and shuffles over to the door. Unlocking the safety latch he opens the door to a large middle aged woman in an old loud print flower dress with slightly graying hair tired up in a bun at the back of her head and small framed eyeglasses.

She is wearing old brown colored stockings, low cut black laced shoes and folding her hands in front of her she looks rather stern.

"Hello, Mrs. Burnside. I was just reading the paper to Nibs. Your remember Nibs, my companion?"

"May I come in? I need to talk to you."

"Of course, after all you are the landlady, so if anyone has a right to come in, you do." Mrs. Burnside walks through the door and stepping over piles of old newspapers and magazines about the floor stands a little way from the couch as Mr. Cuttleworth once again sits back down on the couch.

"Won't you sit down, if you can find a place to sit? I have been meaning to clean the place up, but just haven't gotten around to it being so busy having to read to Nibs all of the time since he insists upon it."

"Thank you, but I'll just stand. I'll come directly to the point. You're over a month behind in your rent. You have been a good tenant always paying your rent on time, but this is the one time you've been late. Why are you late this time? Have you been ill?"

"No, not me, it's my old friend of fourteen years, Nibs. You remember Nibs? Say hello to Mrs. Burnside, Nibs. She is our landlady. She wants to know why I am late in paying the rent."

"Yes, you have introduced me to your cat Nibs a dozen times, but I am not here to talk to you about your cat. I'm here to talk to you about your lateness in paying the rent. Why haven't you paid me the rent in well over month?"

"Well Mrs. Burnside, you see Nibs here was under the weather last month and I had to stay home and care for him."

"What's that got to do with not paying the rent?"

"I couldn't very well go and deposit my social security check at the bank to pay you, because I couldn't leave Nibs."

"You've always paid me by check. Why couldn't you've just paid me by check, just like always?"

"I couldn't because I would have had to deposit my social security check in the bank before I could write you a check."

"In that case you had better go to the bank and deposit your social security check so you can pay your rent. I'll give you five more days to get that check to me or I'll be back and if I have to come back again I may have to take you to court to evict you."

Mrs. Burnside turns around and exits through the door.

"That's what I mean Nibs it seems everybody is greedy for power and money these days. Why in the old days people were happier just to have friends and something to eat. You take yourself Nibs, why you seem to be content with having me as a friend and something to eat. Yes sir Nibs, the world could learn a lot from you on how to be more civilized. What's that Nibs? Yeah, you've right again, old Mrs. Burnside is very greedy when it comes to the rent. Rent this, rent that. Rent, rent, rent, that is all she ever thinks of is the rent. Why when she goes to heaven God will more than likely have her collect the rent for those entering heaven. What's that Nibs? You've right again, she most likely will go to the other place where she will collect the rent for the devil and if they don't pay their rent on time she'll have the devil throw them in the Lake of Fire. What would you do Nibs if you suddenly came in to a lot of money? What's that you say Nibs? You would? You would buy us an island where we would not have to pay rent again? Oh that would be truly wonderful Nibs. But getting a lot of money is wishful thinking as it just can not possibly happen, but it is a nice dream Nibs."

It is five days later near mid afternoon as once again Mr. Cuttleworth is sitting reading to his cat Nibs, "It says here President Hoover has bought his wife a Hoover vacuum cleaner for her birthday after she believed he invented it in their garage. What's that Nibs? Oh yes, I know the newspaper I am reading from is older than you or I, but the point is President Hoover should have not lead his wife to believe he invented the Hoover vacuum cleaner.

If a president misleads his wife then he might also mislead his country and in fact that may have been the reason he got America in to the depression and....,"

Just then a knock is heard on the door. Mr. Cuttleworth gets up and goes to the door to open it and there stands a smartly dressed woman in her thirties.

"Yes, how may I help you?"

The woman answers, "Are you Mr. Cuttleworth?"

"I am and who might you be?"

Woman answering, "My name is Mrs. Sarah Felts, I'm with Social Services but you may call me Sarah. Your landlady Mrs. Burnside called me and said you were having some problems so I have come to see if I might be of some help."

"Well it's not me that has the problems, it is Nibs my cat. Lately he has been under the weather."

"Mrs. Burnside tells me you are over a month behind on your rent and she hasn't seen you go out much lately."

"It seems Mrs. Burnside is kind of nosey isn't she? If I don't go out enough she wonders why; if I'm out too much she wonders why. Now you take Nibs here, he never is nosey; he doesn't wonder why I stay or why I go, he is content to have me as a friend and something to eat."

"Mr. Cuttleworth, I know you love you cat, but the problem that we need to give full attention to giving Mrs. Burnside your usual monthly rental payment."

"Like I told Mrs. Burnside, Nibs was under the weather last month so I had to stay home to care for him and just couldn't go to the bank to deposit my check so that I could write her a check for the rent."

"Maybe you should think about having Social Security directly deposit your check to your bank account by electronic means."

"No, can't do that either. I don't trust the banks to cash my check before I see it. They might claim I didn't have enough money to cover the rent or just cheat me out of part of my money."

"No they wouldn't do that. If someone did they could go to prison for embezzlement."

"Of course they would have to be caught first."

"Maybe I can be of help to you. Why not sign your social security check, give me a deposit slip, so that I could deposit it in the bank for you?"

"I couldn't do that either, I hardly know you. You could cash my check and I'd never see the money from it."

"Mr. Cuttleworth, It's very obvious that you trust no one, however if you don't pay Mrs. Burnside the rent she'll have you evicted, then neither you nor Nibs will have a place to live."

"It isn't that I don't want to pay my rent, it's just that I haven't had a chance to go down to the bank to deposit my social security check yet."

"How do you manage to buy groceries without money and not leaving your apartment?"

"I have plenty of food. I have food saved in case of a nuclear attack by a foreign power. I've been eating that lately."

"Mr. Cuttleworth, I could take you down town right now where you can deposit your social security check in your bank and then you can write a check to Mrs. Burnside to pay you back rent."

"How can you expect me to go out and get in a car with a stranger? You might kidnap me and Nibs would never see me again."

"I have to leave now. Perhaps you should get to the bank soon, so that Mrs. Burnside won't have you evicted."

Sarah Felts then turns around and heads back down the hall from where she had come.

"You know Nibs people talk more about money than they do about caring for others. Here they tell me because I stayed home and took care of you when you were ill that if I don't give old lady Burnside some money you and I would be kicked out on the street. Now isn't that down right ugly when money is more important than a cat under the weather? It is like what it says in the Sunday paper on the front page, President Roosevelt was said to quote that President Hoover was a rich man who was so unconcerned about other people and the economy since he had plenty of money he never saw the depression coming. Yes I know that Nibs I am reading from an old out dated newspaper, but that is not the point Nibs, the point is people love money more than they do their fellow man or cat for that matter."

It is two days later at Mr. Cuttleworth's apartment. A knock is heard on the door. Mr. Cuttleworth answers it and there stands O'Harrah, the neighborhood police officer. Mr. Cuttleworth speaks, "Why O'Harrah what a pleasure it is to see you. Won't you come in and sit down that is if you can find a place to sit?"

"Mr. Cuttleworth unfortunately this is not a social visit. I have in my hand a subpoena for you to appear in the court of Judge Peterson next Monday on the eviction notice."

"What eviction notice? I never received any notice."

"Mrs. Burnside said she gave you a verbal notice."

"Oh that one, I was going to pay the rent, but Nibs got under the weather again, therefore I couldn't deposit my social security check in the bank in order to write a check to Mrs. Burnside to cover the rent."

"I've known you for over twenty years Mr. Cuttleworth and in all that time you have always paid your rent on time. Why now are you unable to do that Sir?"

"Like I said before, old Nibs there wasn't feeling well, Nibs is well over fourteen years old. Now it is said that cats live longer than dogs, but Nibs has had a rough life what with gangs being on the streets, loud music, knifings and robbers everywhere."

"How could that affect a cat?"

"Because he worries so much that something might happen to me that he got ulcers over it."

"Come on Mr. Cuttleworth, surely you can't expect me to believe that, can you?"

"Old Nibs there is a very intelligent cat. He's as smart as some humans."

"What ever, but you had better go to the court because I would hate to return to serve you with an arrest warrant."

"Is there anything I could do in order to not get evicted? If I were to pay the rent now would I still have to move out?"

"If I were you I'd see a lawyer. Now as a matter of fact my lawyer's good and he's also inexpensive too."

"What's his name?"

"Mr. S.L. Wilson. He's in the telephone directory, why not give him a call?"

"Thank you, I'll call him right now."

O'Harrah turns and goes out the door. Mr. Cuttleworth looks through a pile of books on the couch finds the phone directory and looks up the lawyer O'Harrah told him about. Then he dials the number on his telephone, "Hello. Is this Mr. S. L. Wilson the lawyer?" There is a pause before Mr. Cuttleworth goes on, "It is? My friend Officer O'Harrah recommended you to me.

Well I need to see you right away, I have to be in court next Monday and I have to see you before then. What time?

Yes, ten o'clock will be fine. Yes Sir I'll be there on time. See you then."

Mr. Cuttleworth hangs the phone and turning to his cat says,

"You know Nibs I am in all this trouble over helping you. I sure hope you appreciate it because if I hadn't been taking care of you when you were ill I wouldn't be in this mess now."

Mr. Wilson the lawyer is sitting in his dingy-cluttered office. His desk is untidy, papers scattered about. Mr. Wilson is a large heavy set man, balding, clean shaven with close set rather piggish like eyes. He is wearing a wrinkled white Panama suit two sizes smaller than it should be. His white shirt is faded and old. He wears a bright polka dot red tie.

On the little finger of right hand and middle finger he wears gaudy looking diamond rings. In is mouth he has an unlit cigar.

The office walls have a few cheap looking pictures hanging on them. A window overlooks the street as its slat blinds are partially open. There is a closet door on another wall. On the outside doors' frosted window that leads in to his office are the words, "S. L. Wilson, Attorney at Law."

There is a knock at the door and Mr. Wilson says, "Come in." The door opens and Mr. Cuttleworth walks in. Mr. Wilson looking toward the door asks. "Are you the man that called me? Are you Mr. Cuttleworth?"

"I am Sir. I am Kidder Cuttleworth. No middle name."

"Please sit down." Mr. Cuttleworth pulls up a chair next to Mr. Wilson's desk and sits down. Then Mr. Wilson asks Mr.Cuttleworth, "Could you please tell me the whole story of why you have to go to court next Monday?"

"Well my cat Nibs got sick last month and I had to stay with him, I couldn't get to the bank to deposit my social security check so I could make a check out to pay the rent, the reason Nibs was ill was because he was worried about me being on the streets when there is all this crime and now they want to evict me."

"Do I understand you to say; because there is too much crime in the street, you can't pay your rent; and they want to evict you because your cat was sick because he couldn't deposit your social security check and therefore you have no money, am I right so far?"

"Well not quite. My cat was ill. He was ill because there is too much crime. He worried about me. I could not get to the bank because I could not leave him. I had my social security check, but had not cashed it. If I had, had money in the bank I could pay my rent by check. However on the way here I finally deposited it."

"So what you would like me to do is sit with your sick cat so your landlady won't have to walk the unsafe streets while you go and try to pay the rent?"

"No sir, I want to pay the rent before they evict me and want to know if they can still make me move?"

"If you pay the rent before you go to court and the landlady accepts it, the judge can't make you move, but if you offer to pay the rent and the landlady refuses the money, then you won't owe her any and the judge will throw the case out of court, but if your cat tries to pay the rent, your landlady can refuse and the judge will order you evicted, but if the landlady accepts it then your cat can move in and you will be evicted. However if your cat wins in court and you lose, then your cat can get a writ to let you stay providing you pay part of the rent or he can take you to court and get you evicted."

"No, no Mr. Wilson; my cat already lives with me and he is smart, but he doesn't pay any rent."

"Your cat doesn't sound very smart to me not paying his share of the rent, but I'll represent you in court and see what I can do about preventing you from being evicted. Can you ask your cat to go to court with you and speak on your behalf?"

"My cat can't talk so it won't do any good to bring him to court."

"Can he understand you?"

"Yes, he can understand me because we talk the same language."

"Oh so you meow too? Tell me how long have you been meowing?"

"Oh I don't meow. Nibs can speak and understands English."

"English? I never could understand those English. How is it you and he learned to speak like those English? Did you both study in England?"

"Oh no Sir, I meant American English."

"Well why on earth didn't you say so in the first place? I can't afford to have my valuable time wasted on a lot of nonsense and idle talk. So you can understand him and he you then?"

"Yes Sir. And I'm sorry I wasted your time."

"Fine then you can interpret for him, and don't waste any more of my time beating it around the bush as I have a bunch of clients waiting to see me in the waiting room"

"What waiting room? I never saw a waiting room."

"There you go again wasting my precious time with a bunch of silly questions."

"I am truly sorry Sir, but do you think my cat Nibs' testimony in court will help me?

Do you really think it will help my case?"

"If he is your only witness, then I say yes. It is more likely the judge will believe your cat, because animals are not capable of telling lies unless they are skunks, skunks are known to lie. I was once married to a skunk once and she lied all of the time."

"I didn't know they would allow a cat in court?"

"I don't know of any law that says a cat can't testify for its owner unless of course it is a skunk and no judge will allow a skunk in court although some judges are skunks them selves from my own experience."

"So should I try to get a subpoena for my cat Nibs before I go to court next Monday?"

"Yes by all means and hurry up; you only have four days left to do so and today is Thursday. However you might make it today if you hurry."

"Couldn't you do it for me if I paid you extra?"

"I charge twenty-five dollars an hour for humans, but for cat's fifty dollars an hour.

Unless of course he is dog, then I charge thirty dollars an hour for dogs. However I refuse to represent a skunk no matter how much you offer to pay."

"Why is that?"

"Because they stink and tell lies."

"I wasn't asking about skunks."

"And I won't tell you about them either because they stink and are liars."

"I wasn't referring to skunks."

"Because dogs are a wag in, they woof down my every word and don't bark up the wrong tree or whine about my fees."

"I meant why the difference in cats and humans mostly?"

"Because I don't speak their language therefore I have to hire an interpreter to come in and by law we need another interpreter in addition to your self."

"But why can't I interpret for him?"

"The law clearly states that an owner cannot interpret for his cat, because it would be a conflict of interest while taking a brief in a lawyer's office."

"But if I can interpret for him in court I can't see why I can't interpret for him in a lawyer's office?"

"The reasoning behind that is when you are in the court room you are acting for the judge and not for yourself, but when in a lawyer's office then you are acting for yourself."

"Sure that makes sense at least I suppose it does."

"Okay then what's your cat's name?"

"His name is Nibs."

"What's his last name?"

"Same as my last name, Cuttleworth."

"So you officially adopted him, did you?"

"Well no he was a stray kitten I found wandering in alley over fourteen years ago and I just adopted him on my own without doing anything legally about it."

"That will never do! If the judge finds out you illegally adopted that cat you could get yourself in to a world of trouble. Why you could go to prison and get up to forty years at hard labor or possibly even the death penalty. Why it is a very serious crime in this state. But I'll tell you what I'll do, for another fifty dollars I'll draw up the adoption papers to make it all nice and legal."

"Well------okay. But are you quite sure I could go to prison or even get the death penalty just for not legally adopting my cat?"

"Absolutely! It is an old law, been on the books since seventeen seventy two when they burnt people to the stake for having cats they thought might be witches unless they adopted them, then the law classified them as adopted children instead of cats."

"Alright then I won't argue with you because I don't know the laws that well."

"Let's see now; fifty dollars for the adoption papers, twenty-five dollars for my consultation fees, fifty dollars for interpretation fee and fifty dollars for wasting my time. That comes to one hundred and seventy-five dollars, plus twenty-five dollars for the subpoena and fifty-dollars filing fee. Then there's the fifty dollars penalty for your cat not being a dog. Hmmm, let's see, that totals three hundred dollars."

"Wait a minute, how could you charge fifty dollars for the interpretation fees when my cat wasn't here to be questioned? And why are you penalizing my cat for not being a dog? And how was I wasting your time?"

"There you go again wasting my time with too many questions. Now I'll have to add on another fifty dollars to the listed fees bringing a grand total of three hundred and fifty dollars."

"This is totally unfair, but then my friend O'Harrah recommended me to you, so I hope you've good for all of this money. But Nibs isn't here now to agree along with me on all these charges since he and I are partners in everything."

"You were here by proxy for him, so that is the same thing."

"I'll buy that, but where is your interpreter?"

"Oh I stood in proxy for him."

"So how soon do I have to pay you?"

"If you were to pay me today I can fore go the interest fees you would have to pay later if you waited."

"Will you take a check?"

"Sure."

"Then I'll write you check right now, but since I didn't bring my check book I'll need a blank check."

"Let's see, I'm going to have to add secretarial expenses to accept the check and give you a receipt. That comes to fifty more dollars. Then there is the fee for the blank check, which is another twenty-five dollars.

And then there's the fifty dollars for the filing fee on the check. That brings the total to four hundred and seventy-five dollars."

"Wait a minute, where is the secretary?" Now don't tell you're acting as her proxy."

"You're getting smarter, you might make a good attorney someday."

"I'm just too honest for that, but is seems as twenty-five dollars for one blank check is far too much."

"I'm sorry, but I can't sell you one blank check, you will have to take the whole box and then since I had to pay to have them brought over here by a messenger, I had to charge you for that too."

"Okay, but give me the rest of my checks then."

"I'm sorry, but I can't do that since you didn't order them. Now I did order them for my clients, but I have to charge for all of them even if you used only one, that's the law."

"To be sure I certainly don't want to break the law, then hand me one of those blank checks and I'll make you a check out for four hundred and seventy-five dollars."

"Okay and I hope you do well in court next Monday."

"Won't you be there to represent me?"

"Certainly if you wish, but that will be another twenty-five dollars paid in advance."

"What if I was to go to the bank and get you cash, would that make it any cheaper?"

"Not at all, I would have to charge you fifty dollar banking fee expense to put the cash in the bank."

"Alright, alright; I'll write you the check for five hundred dollars."

"Did you want your cat to testify on your behalf?"

"That's what we agreed upon."

"Then that will be another fifty dollars for me to question your cat at the trial, plus fifty dollars for the told tax and fifty dollars for the cut off fee, which brings the total fees to six hundred and fifty dollars."

"You mean to say you charge fifty dollars to question a witness? And what is the told tax?"

"Just cats, and if I told you what the told tax is I would have to charge you another fifty dollars."

"Why just cats?"

"Because I need an interpreter, or like I said, dogs are cheaper. Unless he is a skunk, then I have to charge triple because skunks are known to lie."

"But I don't have a dog or a skunk and I'm going to be the interpreter."

"I know that, but the law requires I charge you fifty dollars for you to be my interpreter."

"How much for an outside interpreter other than myself?"

"There is the research in order to find an outside interpreter, that's fifty dollars; plus the cost of hiring the interpreter, that's another fifty dollars."

"Okay, okay; I'll make you out a check for six hundred and fifty dang dollars, now is there any other charges I don't know about before I write this check out?"

"None that I can think of but if you can think of any let me know so I can add them on.

By the way, if you have no money in the bank won't this check bounce?"

"Like I said, I deposited my last months and this month's social security checks in the bank just before I arrived here early this morning, so it should not bounce."

"Just as long as your money isn't made of rubber or it may bounce, unless it is made of latex as latex doesn't have much bounce to it."

"Can you keep me from getting evicted?"

"I guarantee it as the judge and I are like two eggs in can."

Mr. Cuttleworth writes out the check for six hundred and fifty then hands it to Mr. Wilson. Then states, "Here Mr. Wilson is your check." Mr. Wilson accepts the check saying nothing.

So Mr. Cuttleworth asks "Aren't you going to say anything?"

"If I do I'll have to charge you another fifty dollars."

It's the courtroom of Judge Peterson. The judge who appears to be in his fifties with gray hair wearing silver rimmed glasses, a black judge's smock is medium built.

The courtroom is paneled in light hardwood with three overhead fluorescent lights.

The floor is covered in a dark brown carpet. Behind the judge's bench high on the wall is a framed photographs of the president of the United States and on either side of the judge's bench are the flags of the United States and the state of Indiana. Three large windows framed in white drapes look out on to a busy street. Mr. Cuttleworth, his cat Nibs, his lawyer Mr. Wilson are seated to the left side of the judge's bench before an oak table, landlady Mrs. Burnside and the social worker Sarah Felts are all seated to the right of the judge's bench also before an oak table. The judge speaks (he hasn't any bailiff) "I am the honorable Judge Thomas Peterson, municipal judge for the City of Pleasant Grove, Indiana. Mr. Cuttleworth?" asks Judge Peterson looking toward Mr. Cuttleworth.

"Yes I am Mr. Cuttleworth."

"Would you state your full name?"

"Kidder Cuttleworth, I have no middle name."

"Are you represented by an attorney?"

"I am your honor. I am represented by Mr. Wilson whom is my attorney."

"Mrs. Burnside?"

Mrs. Burnside stands up to speak: "I am Mrs. Burnside."

"And what is your full name?"

"Ima Hedda Burnside."

"Aren't you Mrs. Burnside?"

"Yes I am your Honor."

"Then why did you tell me you're a head of Burnside?"

"No your Honor, my name is Ima Hedda Burnside. Hedda is my maiden name. I was married to Seymour Burnside, but he died five years ago when he was killed in an apartment fire.

Oh it was a dreadful thing and he was only forty two, but he looked more like forty one as he took care of his health, except he did smoke cigarettes and drink beer and as it was he got drunk and accidentally dropped his lighted cigarette on the couch which caught fire and as he slept he died in the fire. We had been married for twenty years and had met in high school. Actually he was going with my best friend Mary Kristmas, but he dropped her on new years and we started dating after that. It was love at first sight. And he surely was a sight, long hair to his waist and a full beard; he looked like Abe Lincoln, except he wasn't as handsome. Oh but did I love Abe Lincoln in grade school, what a handsome dashing man that president was. But my husband Seymour saw more in me and less of Mary. He wanted to be fireman too, but I talked him out of it telling him it was dangerous work and he might get killed in a fire some day, so he took my advice which of course was the wrong advice. But only our side got burned. The neighbors were spared."

"I am not interested in a history lesson of your family."

"I'm sorry your Honor."

"Mrs. Burnside, are you represented by an attorney?"

"No I am not your Honor I could not find an honest one."

"According to the complaint brought by Mrs. Burnside, the plaintiff, Mr. Cuttleworth being the defendant, is more than a month behind in his rent and Mrs. Burnside wants him evicted. Is that correct Mrs. Burnside?

"That is correct your Honor."

"Mr. Cuttleworth, what do you have to say about that?

Mr. Wilson raises his hand as he speaks to the judge, "I will speak for Mr. Cuttleworth since I am his attorney. Mr. Cuttleworth's cat Nibs had been ill and he couldn't leave his side because the crime in the street wouldn't let him go to the bank to deposit his social security check and Mrs. Burnside belonged to the gang that had been terrorizing him so he couldn't pay his rent. Mr. Cuttleworth has a witness, your Honor."

"I object!" exclaims Mrs. Burnside.

"Over ruled! Will Mr. Cuttleworth's witness a Mr. Nibs Cuttleworth come before the bench and be sworn in! Nibs Cuttleworth, please come to the stand!"

"Your Honor, Nibs Cuttleworth is the defendant's cat." injects Mrs. Burnside.

"His cat? I'm sorry Counselor, but I can't allow a cat as a witness."

"What if he is a dog?"

"It matters not I can't allow an animal to be a witness in my courtroom."

"Mr. Cuttleworth is acting as an interpreter for his cat, your Honor."

"I can't help that I just can't have a cat as a witness in a trail."

"Mr. Cuttleworth has assured me that he understands cat language, that his cat in turn understands him and that his cat is a reliable witness who has lived with the defendant for the past fourteen years, and your Honor he isn't a skunk either."

"I am sorry Counselor, but the court cannot accept the testimony of a cat."

"Not even if the cat is put under oath?"

"Not even if the cat is put under oath."

"Your Honor, Pedigree versus Unger, section three, page two hundred and forty-five of the nineteen and sixty second volume of Jensen's law, Judge Hector Wunderbar ruled "that any human who could interpret what an animal said unless of course he was a skunk could be a witness in a trial whereas it has to do with an eviction notice as ruled by the Supreme Court under section six, volume twenty of the nineteen ten revised edition of Littleton's Volume number ten."

"Oh I guess I must have missed that one. Okay you may call your witness, Counselor." Mr. Cuttleworth leans over and whispers in to Mr. Wilson's ear, "You really know your law." Mr. Wilson replies whispering, "Yes, especially when I made that part up."

"Will Nibs Cuttleworth come forward so the court may swear you in?"

"I object your honor. Nibs Cuttleworth is Mr. Cuttleworth's cat, so that would be a conflict of interest."

"Sustained."

"But your Honor, you ruled that Nibs Cuttleworth could testify."

"You didn't tell me that Nibs Cuttleworth was Mr. Cuttleworth's cat. I thought he was a dog or perhaps even a skunk"

"I most certainly did in the very beginning. And I didn't mean to imply he was a dog or a skunk, in fact I do not represent skunks."

"Yes, in the beginning, but after I ruled that the cat could be a witness, you did not inform me that the cat's name was Nibs Cuttleworth or that he even was a cat or a dog for that matter, or that he might have even been a skunk."

"But your Honor the last time I represented a skunk she ended up divorcing me six months later. I'll not represent a skunk."

"I did not imply that Nibs Cuttleworth was a skunk Counselor, but that I did not know rather he was one, or what he was."

"I am sorry your Honor. Mr. Cuttleworth's cat is named Nibs Cuttleworth and I call him as a witness."

"I object." says Mrs. Burnside.

"Over ruled. Call your witness Counselor!"

"Will Nibs Cuttleworth come forward to be sworn in?"

"Counselor, will you ask the defendant, Mr. Cuttleworth to interpret to the witness that he is to testify?"

"Mr. Cuttleworth will you tell your witness to come forward and be sworn in?"

No response from Nibs.

"Your Honor Nibs is shy, can he witness from there?"

"Well alright I'll make an exception this time. Please interpret to your witness the oath after I say it. Mr. Nibs Cuttleworth, do you swear to tell the truth, the whole truth and nothing but the truth so help you God?"

"Nibs, you heard the judge. Do you swear to tell the truth? What's that? Your Honor Nibs said he can't swear to that oath."

"And pray why not?"

"Because Nibs doesn't believe in God, he believes cat created the world. He said if you will replace cat with God in that oath he will except it."

"Oh this is unheard of. Oh very well. Do you Nibs Cuttleworth swear to tell the truth, the whole truth and nothing but the truth so help you cat?"

"Nibs said he will."

"I never heard a peep out of him."

"We talk by mental telepathy."

"This is unheard of. Oh well, I'll accept it this time."

"I object." says Mrs. Burnside.

"On what grounds?" asks Judge Peterson.

"How do we know that they're both not lying?"

"Cats don't have the ability to lie, and both are under oath."

"But your Honor, we can't hear the witness."

"He has an interpreter and that's good enough for me!"

"Mr. Nibs could you tell me your relationship to Mr. Cuttleworth?"

"Nibs said that he is my friend."

Mr. Wilson goes on, "Mr. Nibs, please tell the court why Mr. Cuttleworth was not able to pay the rent last month?"

"Nibs said that he was very ill, that I could not leave him and Mrs. Burnside said it was okay not to pay the rent last month because of it."

"I object." interrupts Mrs. Burnside.

"Over ruled!"

"Mr. Nibs, did you or Mr. Cuttleworth ever explain to Mrs. Burnside that you would catch up the rent as soon as Mr. Cuttleworth could get to the bank and deposit his social security check?"

"Nibs said Mrs. Burnside wouldn't answer the door and refused to accept the rent because she understood about Nibs being ill and felt sorry for him."

"I object." Mrs. Burnside exclaims loudly.

"If I hear another word from you Mrs. Burnside I am going to dismiss this case. You will get your turn."

Mr. Wilson continues, "Mr. Nibs, could you tell me if Mrs. Burnside asked Mr. Cuttleworth for the rent?"

"Nibs said she never did because she was too busy out running the streets and partying with her gang as she was its vice president, I believe it was called the Devil wants his rent Gang or something to that affect."

"Is that all you have to report Mr. Nibs?"

"Nibs said that is about it."

"Would the plaintiff like to cross examine the witness?"

"No thank you, your Honor, I'm not going to ask that lying cat any questions."

"Your witness may be excused, Mr. Cuttleworth."

"Do you wish to testify Mr. Cuttleworth?"

"No your Honor, I believe my witness told it all."

"Mrs. Burnside, I would like to hear your side of the story now. Please stand and raise your right hand." Mrs. Burnside raises her right hand. "Do you swear to tell the truth the whole truth and nothing but the truth so help you God?"

"I do your Honor. And I do not believe a cat created the world, but God. In fact I go to church regularly and if that lying cat would go to church perhaps he wouldn't tell so many fibs."

"Mrs. Burnside, please do not try my patience. This is a court of law, not a circus."

"Forgive me your Honor, I meant no disrespect."

"Would you please give your version of the story?

"Mr. Cuttleworth was over a month behind in his rent and when I went and asked him for it he claimed he had not deposited his social security check in the bank yet in order to make me out my rent check, because he couldn't leave his sick cat alone."

"I object." Mr. Cuttleworth calls out.

"On what grounds?"

"The plaintiff is lying. I never once told her my cat was sick.

I told her my cat was under the weather."

"Is that right Mrs. Burnside?"

"Yes that is true, but I always thought that being under the weather meant one was sick."

"Your honor, the plaintiff is leading the witness." interrupts Mr. Wilson.

"How can the plaintiff be leading the witness when the witness has been dismissed?"

"I withdraw my complaint."

"Mrs. Burnside you may continue."

"Sarah Felts my witness told me she thought that Mr. Cuttleworth had no intentions of paying the rent, so I took him to court instead."

"I object!" exclaims Wilson.

"Sustained."

"But your Honor I am giving testimony."

"That's hearsay. I would like to hear from your witness Mrs. Sarah Felts.

Sarah Felts then stands up.

Would you please state your full name for the record?"

"Sarah Elizabeth Marian Victoria Martha Edwina Anne Felts, your Honor."

"I did not ask you to give me the names of everyone in your family, just your own name."

"But your Honor those are all my names."

"What happened, were you an only child and your mother wanted six other daughters?"

"No your Honor, I was named after my great, great, great grandmother Sarah Elizabeth Marian Victoria Martha Edwina Anne Short."

"Are you sure her last name wasn't Long by any chance, rather than Short?"

"No your Honor, that indeed was her last name."

"Too bad her other names weren't as short.

Would you please stand up and raise your right hand."

Sarah Felts raises her right hand. "Sarah Felts do your swear to tell the truth, the whole truth and nothing but the truth so help you God?"

"I do your Honor. And like Mrs. Burnside I believe God, not a cat created the world."

"I will not have anyone turn my courtroom in to a circus by debating who did or did not create the world."

"I am so sorry I did not mean to turn your courtroom in to a circus. But I am a Christian woman, your Honor."

"Your Honor, then why have you let these two clowns bring this case to court if you do not want your court turned in to a circus?" asks Mr. Wilson.

"Counselor, please control your self in referring to the plaintiff and her witness as clowns."

"I'm sorry your Honor, but the truth sometimes just surfaces by its self."

"Mrs. Burnside you may examine your witness."

"Mrs. Felts, will you tell me your side of the story of what happened when I asked you to go see Mr. Cuttleworth, one of my tenants who was behind in his rent?" asks Mrs. Burnside to Mrs. Felts.

"I had visited Mr. Cuttleworth after Mrs. Burnside had warned him that he was behind in his rent and I tried everything to help him get his social security check cashed, but he said he trusted no one; neither the banks, me or anyone else. Therefore I thought he was trying to avoid even paying the back rent."

"What else did you learn from Mr. Cuttleworth?"

"He talked to his cat and claimed he could speak the cat's language. I felt he was mentally unbalanced and knew that if anyone would believe they could communicate with their cat that they would also avoid paying the rent."

"It is a good thing I made my client pay in advance on my fee then, but then I figured he was unbalanced when he told me the same thing, that he could communicate with his cat." interrupts Mr. Wilson.

"Counselor, you will have your chance to cross examine the witnesses, but thank you for that bit of information."

"Anyway I decided to try to talk Mrs. Burnside out of going back and talking with Mr. Cuttleworth, because I figured he was mentally unbalanced and she wouldn't get anywhere with him."

"Is that all you have to say Mrs. Felts?"

"Yes your Honor."

"Do you have any further questions for Mrs. Felts, Mrs. Burnside?"

"Not at this time your Honor."

"Counselor, do you have any questions for either Mrs. Burnside's witness or Mrs. Burnside herself?"

"No your Honor, but I was wondering if Mr. Cuttleworth is supposed to be mentally unbalanced because he said he talked to his cat, when you being the judge would allow the cat to testify as Mr. Cuttleworth's witness?"

"Good point Counselor, but then you were insistent yourself that the cat testify."

"Does anyone else have anything to say? Do you Mrs. Burnside?"

"No your Honor."

"Do you Mrs. Felts?"

"No your Honor."

"Do you Counselor?"

"No your Honor."

"Do you Mr. Cuttleworth?"

"No your Honor."

"Then I guess I'm ready for my ruling."

"You didn't ask if Nibs had anything else to say your Honor."

"Look Mrs. Felts made it quite clear to me that anyone who believed they could communicate with a cat was mentally unbalanced, so Mr. Cuttleworth, do you want me to show the court I am mentally unbalanced by asking your cat anymore questions?"

"No your Honor, but I can interpret for you."

"No thank you. So if no one has any more questions I'll make my judgment in this case. Mr. Cuttleworth, you are to pay up all of your back rent to Mrs. Burnside immediately and then move out within three days of paying the rent, and take your cat with you.

We don't want any more trouble making cats at Mrs. Burnside's apartments.

Case closed."

It is the next day. Mr. Cuttleworth is back at his apartment packing his things in preparation to moving after paying his back rent to Mrs. Burnside, when there is a knock at the door. Mr. Cuttleworth walks over to the door and upon opening it sees police officer O'Harrah standing at the door. Before Mr. Cuttleworth can open his mouth to ask why O'Harrah is there, O'Harrah himself speaks to Mr. Cuttleworth, "Mr. Wilson wants to see you right away. Your cousin Pepper Schmidt died and Nibs has been named in the will. You are to go over to see Mr. Wilson at one o'clock this coming afternoon to hear the reading of the will."

"Really? Are you serious? Nibs has been named in my cousin Pepper Schmidt's will? Must have left him some kitty litter. Nibs could sure use some good kitty litter. When I was a little tyke they only used sand in the place of kitty litter. Boy, did the litter boxes ever stink! In fact it stunk up the whole house. Yes Sir, they certainly make better kitty litter now. Nibs sure could use some too."

"I personally don't know what cousin Pepper Schmidt left Nibs. He just sent me over here to tell you hurry and get to his office by one o'clock this afternoon to hear the reading of the will because Nibs was named in the will. And oh, leave Nibs here. You go alone."

"Was I mentioned in the will too?"

"I don't know. I have no idea whatsoever is said in the will. But you need to get there on time. Maybe when you get back and I get off duty I can finish helping you pack."

"So it's talking will is it, old cousin Pepper must have recorded it on tape."

"What I meant was I neither saw the will or did Mr. Wilson read it to me."

"Were you named in the will also?"

"No I was not. As a matter of fact I never knew you had a cousin by the name of Pepper Schmidt."

"I don't have a whole lot of cousins left. Pepper had two brothers and a sister.

There was his older brother Jack Schmidt who kept to himself a lot and not too many people knew him. In fact if you ever asked anyone if they knew him they probably would have replied they didn't know Jack Schmidt.

Old Jack was an inventor too. He invented the tubeless tube, a clock that watched you rather than you watched it. An alarm clock that woke you up by giving boring sermons on the bad habit of over sleeping, over eating and it even nagged you like some one's mother in law. He also invented a door bell that if no one was home would tell you so, but that didn't go over too well because houses that used it were burglarized far too often.

Invisible cigarettes for people trying to quit smoking thereby they would spend so much time trying to find their pack of invisible cigarettes that they lost all desire to smoke after a while. He also invented a pencil that wouldn't write thereby you could never make a mistake in misspelling a word and an electric eraser for people who make a lot of mistakes writing they could turn it on and leave it on and it would continuously erase your mistakes. Then there was his brother Luce Schmidt. He gambles a lot and runs around with lots of different women. Luce can't keep any money for long and his brother Pepper said he would never leave him any money because he was too loose with his money.

And Jack is wealthy in his own right. Then of course there's Honey Pott his sister.

She was married to old Phil Wypout the toilet paper millionaire. He died and left her his business and all his assets.

Of course with Honey Pott's high living she soon wiped out Phil Wypout's money and in desperation finally sold most of his shares of his toilet paper company to Usset and Flushet, the second largest toilet paper company.

Honey Pott took after her mother. Her mother Lill Pott was the daughter of P. Pott, one of the partners of the soup company Pee, Porridge and Pott, the soup label of Nine Days Old. Lill spent her money as fast as her father gave it to her and as a result she passed on that trait to her daughter Honey Pott. Honey Pott had a twin brother also that died at birth, Roney Schmidt, Honey and Roney. I'll bet Roney would never have turned out like his sister had he lived. Cousin Pepper was in the portable potty out house business.

He started out with a few hand made one hole jobs. At first business stunk. I visited him a couple of times and his business seemed to be going down the toilet until I introduced him to Nibs."

"So after he met Nibs what happened?"

"It's very likely, I told Cousin Pepper, that Nibs speaking through me could give him the solution for his business problems, and I also mentioned that Nibs was very intelligent and wise. At first Cousin Pepper didn't believe me."

"So how did he happen to change his mind?"

"Well Nibs told him through me what to do on turning his portable potty out houses into a paying business. I then told Cousin Pepper that he would do well to accept the advise as he had nothing to lose. Cousin Pepper seemed to think since his business was going down the sewer that I was right, so he took Nib's advice."

"Didn't your Cousin Pepper have a wife and kids?"

"No, he had a hot temper, he couldn't get along with a woman well enough to marry one.

Now he had many girl friends, but of course being true to his nature he never kept one for long on account of his hot temper."

"Were there any cousins that might have gotten his inheritance?"

"Well there was Cousin Hardin Schmidt. He was married to a Chinese heiress. She was the heir to the Chinese tea company Tea Fall Two. Of course he is rich already. Now you take Honey Pott, more than likely she will expect to have Pepper will her all his money. But she never got along with him, he told me once that he and his sister weren't even on speaking terms."

"Why was that?"

"She was a lazy no good gold digger who thought the world owed her a living. She tried to scamming Cousin Pepper to give her half the business even though she never did a lick of work toward helping her brother put his business together."

"It's quite possible, her being his only sister and being broke might end up getting most of his estate."

"If he had stayed in the portable potty out house business it would have been the perfect business for someone with her attitude, but be as is may, he sold most of his stock for several millions of dollars before he retired which had made him very wealthy and so that was his final state when he more than likely passed away."

"What sort of advice did Nibs give to your cousin?"

"One thing Nibs told him was to change the name of his company from Aim to Please to Schmidt House Manufacturing as Dee Wight House was Pepper's silent partner."

"He had a silent partner?"

"Yes, Dee Wight couldn't hear nor speak."

"Oh he was deaf and dumb then?"

"No he wasn't dumb. He was the brains behind Pepper's company."

"So Nibs advice saved his company then?"

"Of course that that was a real big relief to Cousin Pepper when his sales shot up right through the roof even though his out houses had tin roofs"

"Outside of her being a gold digger, what else might have kept your Cousin Pepper from getting along with his sister?"

"Even as children Honey always wanted everything her way even when she never lifted a finger to help Pepper. She would take his toys without asking then would tell him that he was the baby of the family and everything should be hers."

"I see, so she was always putting up a stink then?"

"Absolutely, Pepper would try every way to please her, but there was just no way she could be pleased; why if he had brought her in to his business she would have wiped him out."

"How dose she get by?"

"Well before she met Wypout she was married to Sess Poole."

"What kind of business was he in?"

"Old man Sess Poole sold septic tanks, but Honey Pott drained all his savings wiping him out too. Old Sess had, had enough of her and divorced her. That's when Honey Pott met Phil Wypout."

"So then you're saying your Cousin Honey married a Wypout, that's incredible, but wasn't he nearly wiped out himself during the seventies?"

"He certainly was, but he came back two ply strong."

"Surely you must mean two fold strong?"

"No, he came out with two ply toilet paper and it kept him in business."

"So does Cousin Honey still own any part of Wypout?"

"Not any more, with her high wasteful living style she wiped out Wypout!"

"I suppose she is broke now and down to her last dollar?"

"Yes, she is down to her last roll."

"You'd best be getting over to Mr. Wilson's office."

It is just seconds away from one o'clock in Mr. Wilson's cluttered office.

Mr. Cuttleworth has just entered and is seated just a way off from Mr. Wilson's desk.

A medium built woman of forty wearing a wide brimmed black floppy hat with a short black veil hanging from the brim of her hat, a tight short black dress above her knees, black nylon stockings, imitation diamonds covering the top of a pair of black high heel shoes, and a carrying a black purse studded with more imitation diamonds head in her hands before her. She is wearing a fox fur collar around her neck. Her face is painted up to look more like a woman of the night rather than a proper lady. Her hands with their long bright crimson nails are adorned with two imitation diamond rings set in gold bands on her right hand Mr. Wilson sitting behind his cluttered desk piled high with papers in a haphazard condition shuffles several pages of papers, then he speaks to the woman before him, Mrs. Honey Pott Wypout and Mr. Cuttleworth although a part from each other are seating patiently to hear the reading of the late Pepper Schmidt's will.

"I am Mr. Shyster Leland Wilson as you might know. I am an attorney at law and my prices are reasonable, in fact down right inexpensive and cheap too.

If you should ever need the presents of a good attorney I am at your service twenty four hours a day, seven days a week except on Saturday and Sunday and only between the hours of 8am to 5 pm Monday through Friday, except on holidays where I am usually not here unless it's an emergency in which case I'm not available unless there is extra money in it, in which case I'll be here as long as you are willing to pay me in cash up front.

I am the executor of the late Pepper Schmidt's last will & testament in which I'll be reading shortly."

"I'm not interested in you promoting your services; can you just get on with it?"

"Of course Mrs. Wypout, so if you and Nibs' representative are ready I'll begin."

"I just don't understand why this Nibs couldn't come himself? What reason did he have for sending some one in his place?" quizzes Honey Pott.

"Nibs is Mr. Cuttleworth's cat."

"His cat? What do you mean his cat?"

"Don't you know what a cat is? It's a feline."

"A cat? My brother named some worthless cat in his will?"

"Nibs is not worthless! The fact is if anyone fits that description it's you Cousin Honey. You wiped out your poor departed husband's fortune after he worked so hard building up one of the largest toilet paper companies." Exclaims Mr. Cuttleworth his face flushed with anger.

"That my dear Cousin Kidder is none of your business, it was my money to do with as I saw fit!"

"Yeah right! So you saw fit to wipe out Wypout. I'll just bet old Phil Wypout rolled over in his grave several times."

"Please restrain yourselves from arguing and let's get on with the reading of this will." injects Mr. Wilson.

"Oh dear Brother Pepper I miss him so much. I loved my dear brother with all my heart."

"You don't even have a heart, so how could you love Cousin Pepper with all your heart?"

"He was my brother and I was closer to than you ever were."

"You were much more closer to his money than you were ever to him. For example where were you when he was starting out in business?"

"I was there to lend a hand."

"You certainly were, to lend him a hand in wasting all of his money."

"Can't we just get on to letting me read the will? The two of you can argue later on your own time." Says Mr. Wilson in frustration.

"Yes, please do get on with it. I have others things I must do yet today." replies Mr. Cuttleworth.

"I Pepper Mill Schmidt being of sound mind, but not necessarily sound body do hereby leave to my only sister my original portable potty outhouse because she is full of it.

She can quite easily fill it. And to my dear friend and advisor, Nibs Cuttleworth whose advice made me rich beyond my imagination I leave the rest of my entire fortune and assets. I name my cousin, Kidder no middle name Cuttleworth as guardian and executor of Nibs Cuttleworth for the rest of Nibs' life. And should Nibs pass away before his guardian, all of the remaining fortune I leave here-with shall go to a feline chartable organization."

"That filthy cat gets everything? I can't believe that worthless no account brother mine would leave his billions to a no account flea bag cat!"

"If you weren't a woman I'd punch you right in the nose for that remark! It is for sure that Honey Pott is the wrong name for you! It should have been named Vinegar Pott! Maybe if you had not called Nibs such unspeakable names he might have given you a vacant lot in which to set your out house on! But now I'll advise against such a drastic move. You are not worthy to have anything more than your brother's first out house!"

"My brother, the toad won't get away with this! And that no good cat has not heard the last of me!"

"The will concludes; I further state that should Kidder no middle name Cuttleworth pass away before Nibs Cuttleworth, a new executor and guardian shall be named by my friend and attorney, Mr. Wilson whose rates are reasonable and he is inexpensive too. So concludes this will."

"Has my cousin Pepper already been buried?"

"He is to be buried tomorrow afternoon at Spooky Hollow Cemetery over in Pleasant Grove, Indiana. As his sister, Mrs. Honey Wypout, how would you like him buried?'

"I don't care if you bury him face down, upside down or standing him on his head!

He can't do this to me! I am his sister!"

"I'm afraid he already did, and there is nothing that can change the will now."

"Maybe you can rent out the out house he left you, then you will at least have some sort of income."

"I'll contest the will through court first! I'll hire the best lawyer in the state of Indiana! I'll take it all of the way to the supreme court if I have to!"

"I'm the best lawyer in the state of Indiana, and you don't have enough money to hire me. In fact I understand you are penniless. Dead broke. You haven't any money.

In order to contest your brother's will, it will take a lot of money. Give it up, take the out house and be grateful he even left you that.

Someday that portable potty outhouse could become a priceless antique worth millions. Hold on to it and perhaps you can sell it in your old age and become rich from its sale."

"Oh all of this may be funny to you, Mr. Wilson, but you haven't heard the last of me yet! Just you wait and see!"

"I won't hold my breath. That's it, Mrs. Wypout. I'll have your portable potty outhouse delivered this afternoon at your front door."

"My front door? I don't want it! Give it to some one else!"

"I'm afraid I can't do that. As your late brother's attorney I am only carrying out the wishes of your late brother, and therefore I must have the portable potty outhouse he left you delivered at your place of residence. What you do with it after that is strictly up to you."

"But I live in a very fancy exclusive neighborhood of upper high class homes. What will the neighbors say?"

"That it looks like Mrs. Wypout has just taken delivery of a new guest cottage." Mr. Cuttleworth quips.

"Oh you think that is funny do you Cousin Kidder? You won't be laughing when I contest the will."

"You can leave now. I'll be busy making the arrangements for Nibs Cuttleworth to receive his share of the estate. So you'll have to excuse me." says Mr. Wilson to Honey Pott.

"If Cousin Pepper had left you any money, you would have squandered that away too."

"You'll not get away with this! Somehow I'll get my hands on that money and that no account animal won't get one red cent! Mark my words, the battle isn't over yet!"

"At least you're one battle axe that doesn't know when to quit. Nibs might possibly give you a couple of bucks so you can at least have part of your dream come true of getting your hands on that money."

"Now if each of you will sign this paper here (Mr. Wilson lays a paper before Mr. Cuttleworth and Honey Pott Wypout at the foot of his desk and then offers them the use of his pen) I'll hand over to each of you a copy of the will."

"I'll not sign anything until I hire myself an attorney to contest the will!"

"Suit yourself, but if you don't have any money, how do you plan to hiring an attorney?"

"I suppose it's always possible that you could trade the out house Cousin Pepper left you for the services of an attorney."

"Oh very funny Mister Fancy Pants! But I'll have the last laugh! I'll show you all!"

"Why yes, you could always sit in your out house and have your fat fanny self a hearty good laugh at that." Mr. Wilson chuckles to himself.

As Honey Wypout rises and stalks out of the room in to the hall of the building in a huff, she yells out to those behind her,

"You haven't heard the last of me Wilson and Cuttleworth!"

Then she turns and slams the door so hard she shatters the glass in it.

"I've known her all life. The only thing she cares about is money. Lots of it. But she never holds on to it for long to keep any."

"Without money to hire an attorney you won't have to worry about her, it's quite likely you never will see from her again."

"Well good enough. If that's all I have to sign I had best sign that paper then and hurry back to our apartment to tell Nibs the good news.

Nib's has been left there all by his self. By the way did he receive very much money? Is there enough to buy him some decent kitty litter?"

"According to my information your cousin invested his money in a lot of different things making him a multi-billionaire. Nibs will receive fifty million dollars in cash, a country manor house of three rooms in Pleasant Grove, a small summer cottage of one hundred and sixty rooms in the south of France. A small vacation cabin of two hundred and thirty rooms in southern Oregon. Ten new pink and gold portable potty outhouses, three ten story dog hotels and twenty five thousand acres of prime real estate land fit for donkeys in Montana with two trees on it. Four twenty story office buildings here in Pleasant Grove each with its own built in elevator operated by a hand crank. Two apartment houses facing each other by two feet and a bean beer brewery also here in Pleasant Grove, plus several stocks and bonds valued at two hundred million. Ten rich pumping, but leaking oil wells in eastern New Mexico. An abandoned clock store in Corona, New Mexico with five thousand clocks. An eighty room ranch house with an old out house out back with a hundred and seventy five thousand acres in Why, Arizona, two gold mines in No Lode, California, a tour bus service in northern Siberia with a salt mine, two run down worthless airlines and a fifty five percent interest in the Schmidt House Manufacturing Company. His total assets including the fifty million dollars cash comes to over three hundred billion dollars and nine cents, actually closer to four hundred billion and nine point three cents."
"Fifty million dollars! That could buy the best kitty litter there is with gold dust mixed in it! Nibs is rich! His worries are over for good! Hurrah! Hurrah! I've got to thank you Mr. Wilson! Oh thank you!"

"Just doing my job. I'll take care of all the arrangements and have all of the monies and the assets turned over to Nibs immediately. I'll be calling on you shortly."

"By the way, how did my cousin die?"

"It was a rather strange death. Your cousin had sold forty five percent of his portable potty outhouse business to stockholders and retained fifty five percent, then he semi retired.

But your cousin liked to come around and inspect his portable potties none the less from time to time. It was just on such an occasion that he inspected one that was perched atop a steep hill above a flax seed mine when the manager of the company, a man that went by the name of Big Bad John had just hiked up that hill from a mine below where the portable potty outhouse served the fifty miners working in that hard seed mine.

Anyway Big Bad John being all out of breath from hiking up the hill happened to lean on that very outhouse while your dear departed cousin was inside inspecting it. Now mind you Big Bad John was a big, big, big man, he stood over six foot six and weight in over three hundred pounds. It was his weight that caused the outhouse to roll down the hill with your cousin in it. The sad state of affairs when they discovered your cousin's mangled body inside that outhouse at the bottom of the hill was that everybody else's business was covered over your cousin. Now your cousin didn't stick his nose in other people's business, but other people's business was stuck in his nose cutting off his breathe and was the result of his demise. Strange too, only two weeks prior to this he came to me with a strange tale.

He claimed to have had a dream that he was driving one of his portable potties in the mountains at a high rate of speed and lost control on a sharp curve and plunged down a mountainside and he died upon reaching the bottom. Can you imagine your cousin coming up with such a tale? And at his age speeding, why he should have known better.

Why I knew he had to be lying. I mean come on, people don't go around driving portable potties. Why for one thing the motor vehicle department wouldn't allow them on the highway, they are much too light and the smell would distract other drivers.

Anyway after he told me that ridiculous tale I told him perhaps he should have me draw up a will for him as I was trying to humor him and make a fast buck too out of the bargain, in which he agreed and I did. And it was barely two weeks later he died in that most unfortunate accident when he rolled off that steep hill on a mountainside in that portable potty. I wished I had believed him now. Why you would never get me driving one of his portable potties. They are just too unsafe, and besides I'll bet they don't have much trade in value as most of those little sports jobs don't anyway. Well I need to take care of getting Mrs. Wypout's portable potty outhouse delivered today and see to it Nibs' estate is signed over to him. So if there are no more questions I'll have to bid you a good day."

Mr. Cuttleworth is back at his apartment and has told Nibs the good news about the inheriting fifty million dollars and the assets that went with it. Mr. Wilson has asked O'Harrah to go sit with Nibs

Cuttleworth to be there in case Nibs goes in shock from his good fortune. O'Harrah has come over to Mr. Cuttleworth's apartment and is now sitting on an old armchair that moments before was stacked with old magazines and newspapers. Mr. Cuttleworth sits on the couch with Nibs cuddled up in his lap purring loudly.

"Just think Nibs, you're a multi-billionaire. Richer than anyone in Pleasant Grove. Maybe even the whole state of Indiana. What's that you say? Sure, you can buy anything you want now. You have fifty million dollars and cats don't have to pay inheritance tax on their inheritance. And you've also worth close to four hundred billion. Why you've worth almost a half of a trillion dollars Nibs."

"You know you may not have to move now."

"Why is that?"

"Mrs. Burnside is only leasing this building from the real owners. Her lease ran out just today. The building is for sale or lease. The owners would rather sell it than lease it anyway. Now that Nibs is rich he could buy it and you wouldn't have to leave."

"Did you hear that, Nibs? This building is for sale by the real owners. What's that? You say go ahead and buy it. Alright then, I'll buy it. We won't have to move now Nibs."

"But you'll have to hurry before Mrs. Burnside renews her lease this afternoon as she plans to."

"Since Mr. Wilson is taking care of putting everything in Nibs' name with me as executor and guardian as we speak, I'll go see the owners right away."

"Perhaps I should get on then and get back to work."

"Nibs said he is going to need a body guard now that he is a rich tycoon, and he would like to hire you as his body guard if you want the job?"

"That is very nice of Nibs to offer me the job. Now what will my salary be on that?"

"Nibs says five thousand dollars a month, plus room and board and expenses."

"Wow! Tell Nibs I except. I will first have to give the police department thirty days notice though as it's in my contract with them."

"Alright you can give them your notice, but as of now you've hired and work Nibs. Would you go tell Mr. Wilson, Nibs wants to hire him on as his personal private attorney at twice what he brings in a month now. Also being a cop, investigate him to see how much he now makes so he can't scam Nibs in giving more than he is worth."

"Yes Sir. And you might tell Nibs from now on I'll address him as Mister Nibs since he is going to be my employer. I worked for the department for many years, but never expected to be offered a job like Mister Nibs gave me. Wait until I tell my girl friend Maggie. She always said being a police officer was dangerous, but a secure job with peanuts as pay and little benefits. But won't she be surprised when I tell her I am going to work for multi-billionaire as his body guard."

"Oh by the way O'Harrah, Nibs said for you to call Mr. Wilson right now to arrange for Nibs to buy this building immediately before Mrs. Burnside has a chance to force us to move."

"Tell Mr. Nibs I'll go do that right now." O'Harrah then gets up and exits through the door.

"Well Nibs it looks like we might as well unpack then because before the sun sets you will be the new owner of this building, then no one can make us move. And you know what Nibs?, I'll bet there is no one richer in Indiana than you are. Why with your money you could buy the entire city of Pleasant Grove."

It is the next morning in Mr. Cuttleworth's apartment. O'Harrah and Mr. Wilson are there. The evening before Nibs had Mr. Cuttleworth arrange to have the owners of the building come to Mr. Cuttleworth's apartment with their attorney after Mr. Cuttleworth gave them a check for the amount they were asking for the tenement building.

The owners of the building then turned the deed of the property over to Mr. Cuttleworth to keep for Nibs. A knock is heard at the door. Mr. Cuttleworth gets up from his still cluttered couch and ambles over to the door and opens it. There stands Sarah Felts.

"If you are ready I'll take you and Nibs to the shelter."

"We aren't going to any shelter. We are staying here and you had better leave because this building has been taken over by Nibs."

"Now Mr.Cuttleworth, don't get excited, I am not here to harm you. I am only trying to help you. You know you have to vacate the building."

O'Harrah upon over hearing the conversation at the door arises and walking over to the door tells Mrs. Felts, "Mr. Cuttleworth is telling you the truth. I was sent over here by Mr. Wilson the attorney awhile ago. Nibs just inherited a three hundred billion dollar estate and Mr. Cuttleworth was made executor and guardian. Nibs bought this building from the owners just a short time ago. Mrs. Burnside was only leasing it from the former owners. I and Mr. Wilson there have been hired by Nibs as his body guard and personal attorney respectfully."

"Oh I'm so happy for you Mr. Cuttleworth and your cat Nibs too. If there is anything I can ever do for you please let me know."

"Well you're pretty two faced. You had better leave this building right away as Nibs hired O'Harrah here as his body guard and if you don't leave right now the first official act O'Harrah will be ordered to do is to throw you out of here."

"I'm leaving! I'm leaving right now!" Sarah hurries away and Mr. Cuttleworth closes the door behind her.

It is a several days later. O'Harrah has quite his job and is working full time for Nibs. All the legal papers transferring money and assets of the estate of Pepper Schmidt have been signed and turned over to the care of Mr.Cuttleworth. There is loud knocking at the door. O'Harrah gets up from a new comfortable chair in the now cleaned up apartment with new furnishings and opens the door for Mr. Cuttleworth who is enjoying watching a new sixty inch TV screen. When he opens the door there stands Mrs. Burnside with her arms folded over her breast and a stern look on her face.

"Is Mr. Cuttleworth here?"

"Yes he is."

"Well he was suppose to be out of here more than a week ago!

I'm going to get in touch with Judge Peterson and have a warrant served on Mr. Cuttleworth for contempt of court for going against the judge's order of eviction and not vacating his apartment within three days of paying his back rent! The building has been sold to new owners and I'm inclined to believe they will back me on this in getting Mr. Cuttleworth and his cat forcibly removed from this building by the police and perhaps Mr. Cuttleworth will go to jail and his cat taken away from him."

Mrs. Burnside says in a huff.

Mr. Wilson upon hearing Mrs. Burnside's raised voice above the

TV gets up and walks over to the door.

"You can't have that order enforced. Nibs bought the building from the owners and Mr. Cuttleworth is Nibs guardian, so he has every right to be here, but you don't."

Mr. Cuttleworth upon hearing the commotion gets up and shows Mrs. Burnside the deed.

"Yes and Nibs said he wants you out of his building in three days or he is going to Judge Peterson and have you evicted."

"Where on earth did your cat Nibs get that kind of money to buy this building? He must have stolen it"

"Even though it's none of your business, Nibs inherited a three hundred billion dollar estate nearly ten days ago from a late billionaire cousin of mine. And with part of his inheritance he had Mr. Wilson purchase this building within two hours of the lease running out. So you have been living here the past ten days rent free and in arrears."

"Nibs is the new owner? I'm sorry, I did not know. What if I pay him rent? Will he let me stay then?"

"Nibs said since you believe anyone who communicates with cats is mentally unbalanced, that he doesn't want you staying in his building because he thinks you're unbalanced."

"But I haven't anywhere to go."

"Maybe you can get a hold of Sarah Felts. She can help you go in to a shelter."

"Oh please let me stay I'll mop your floors and be your maid."

"Nibs said you were the manager, but since he now owns the building that you are arrears in your rent and if you don't pay it up in three days he is taking you to court and have you evicted."

"I know where you can get an inexpensive lawyer." O'Harrah quips.

"I'm not for hire, I work full time for Mr. Nibs now and he pays me a lot more than I could make had I stayed in private practice."

"I wasn't thinking of you. I was thinking of Mr. Cuttleworth, he seems like a better lawyer than you are."

"If you want to stay however Nibs says you can move in to the basement at five hundred dollars a month."

"I won't stay here if I have to move in to the basement. It's full of rats and cockroaches. I want you to know Mr. Cuttleworth that I am sorry I had to evict you, but I was only doing my job."

"Nibs said he is sorry too, but he too is only doing his job. And as for being full of rats and cockroaches Nibs said you should feel right at home with creatures of your own ilk."

Mrs. Burnside turns and stomps away.

"O'Harrah, Nibs said you can have the rest of the afternoon off and take his new stretch limousine for a drive in the country. Oh, and here (reaching in to his wallet and pulling two bills from it hands it toward O'Harrah) is two one hundred dollar bills. Nibs said take your girl friend Maggie out to dinner on him."

"Why thank you Mr. Nibs. Have a nice day, Mr. Nibs."

"Nibs said your welcome. Say, Mr. Wilson, Nibs said he wants to find a big empty building to buy, then have it completely remodeled in to small apartments some place nearby to let homeless people live in it for free. But Nibs says if either Sarah Felts or Mrs. Burnside wants to move in to charge them five thousand dollars a month unfurnished and they have to furnish their own cockroaches too."

"Yes Sir. Tell Mr. Nibs I'll take care of it right away."

Mr. Wilson leaves and Mr. Cuttleworth and his cat Nibs are alone once again.

Mr. Cuttleworth picks up an old newspaper lying on the couch, opens it and says,

"You know Nibs, things used to really be bad. I'm reading here where Japan has bombed Pearl Harbor. What's that you say? Well sure I know it's an old paper, but times were bad in them days for everybody. Yes Nibs I know that, for us too, but not anymore Nibs, you're a multi-billionaire and I work for you and you and I are never going to see bad times again. What's that you say? You're right, got to get us a maid to come in here, clean this place up and exchange all of these old magazines and newspapers for some new ones with better news too, like cat inherits outhouse fortune. What's that Nibs? Sure, you're the boss, I'll shut up and let you do all the talking.

After all you're the boss Nibs."

CHAPTER TWO

NIBS GOES TO LONDON

It is two weeks later. Nibs' and Mr. Cuttleworth's apartment have been totally remodeled in to a very swanky high class apartment. There is fine expensive furnishings placed in it. Dozens of construction workers are remodeling the other apartments in the building while Nibs has temporary placed all the tenants in one his other apartment buildings across town with the understanding that their rental rates would not go up but down by a hundred dollars a month. Nibs has hired on several new employees; a private secretary who is a short five foot four rather plump woman of about twenty two years old with short blond hair done in ringlets.

She has on a pink bright color flowered dress, high-heel pink shoes, pink nylons, and has gaudy looking rings on all her fingers. She wears several bracelets on each arm including an expensive looking rhinestone watch on her right arm and a string of fake pearls around her neck. Her make up is almost clown like, her lips bright red, heavy rouge on both cheeks, blue eye shadow and eyebrows. In her right hand she holds a long ivory cigarette holder with a long unlit cigarette in it. She also carries a small tablet and rhinestone studded pen to take notes with. Her name is Marcia. There is also a valet named Bentley, he appears to be around forty, clean shaven, lean face, brunette hair, about five foot eight. He wears a tan two piece suit, yellow shirt, red bowtie, brown tassel loafers.

Tracy his nurse is of thirty years of age, is around five foot six, short brunette under an old style white nurse's cap.

She has a rather pretty face against an all white old fashion nurse's uniform; white dress, white cape, white lace up pumps and white stockings. She is of slender built. Also in attendance at Nibs' apartment is O'Harrah. Wilson is absent. His servants are all comfortably seated in the new leather bound chairs and couches of Nibs' newly decorated and furnished apartment.

He has also had Mr. Wilson purchase for him a large sea going yacht that he keeps in the New York harbor. And even a private plane to fly him anywhere he wishes to go.

"Nibs has asked me to have you all here together because Nibs said he needs a long vacation away from here aboard his new yacht. He said he actually has never had a vacation up until now"

"Does the master have any place in mind?" asks Bentley.

"Nibs said he needs to try out his new yacht, the Cat Fish to travel abroad."

"To travel with a broad you say?" O'Harrah quips in good humor.

"O'Harrah, as a former policeman you shouldn't make those kind of jokes about women." Marcia says in a huff her arms folded over her breast.

"Nibs said if he wanted a broad he would get a pussy cat to keep him company. Nibs said he wants to go to London to see the sights."

"Well I'm worried that a long sea voyage might make Mr. Nibs terribly sea sick." Tracy says with concern.

"It all depends on what he sees." quips O'Harrah good naturally.

"I was referring to the ocean."

"So was I."

"How soon does the master wish to leave?" asks Bentley.

"Nibs said the sooner the better. Or either the better the sooner, or which ever comes first."

"Won't we all need visas? asks Marcia.

"Either that or a Master Card." quips O'Harrah.

"I meant passports."

"Nibs said he knows we need passports and Marcia I want you to get Mr. Wilson on the phone and tell we all need passports."

"Which ports will we be passing?"

"How should I know, I have never been out of the state of Indiana, let alone across the ocean."

"Then why did you ask me to ask Mr. Wilson which ports we will be passing?"

"Look, by passports I mean those little certificates one has to have in order to pass from one port of one country to the port of another country."

"Oh you mean tickets to travel by ship?"

"No I mean passports. Oh just call Mr. Wilson and tell him Nibs said you are to ask him to get us passports."

"You want me to ask Mr. Wilson to call Mr. Nibs and ask him we need passports?"

"My goodness, some secretary you are. Hmm, just call Mr. Wilson and tell him we need passports. Believe me he will know what you are talking about even if the rest of us do not because he knows well the language of double talking better than anyone I have ever met."

"How soon do you want me to get him?"

"Nibs said right away."

"By telephone or in person?"

"By telephone!"

Marcia goes over to the telephone, picks it up and dials Mr. Wilson's number, there is a pause for a few seconds, and then Marcia speaks in the mouth piece, "Mr. Wilson? This is Marcia, Mr. Nibs' secretary, Mr. Nibs wants to go to London on his yacht, the Cat Fish." There's a few seconds pause before Marcia continues, "Yes that's right, London. Anyway he wants you to arrange passports for all of us." There's another pause, then,

"I don't know Sir, I'll ask him. Mr. Nibs, Mr. Wilson wants to know how many is going to be going to London with you."

"Nibs said myself, he, O'Harrah, you, Bentley, Mr. Wilson him self, Tracy his nurse, and Howard his chauffeur."

Marcia speaks again on the phone: "Hello Mr. Wilson, are you still there? I'll ask him, Mr. Nibs, Mr. Wilson would like to know why you want to bring Howard your chauffeur along when you can probably hire a limousine while in London? He says he says he is able to hear you."

"Nibs said he doesn't trust those London drivers, they drive on the wrong side of the road and their steering wheels are even on the wrong side of their cars. He wants his own chauffeur driving him where ever he goes."

Marcia speaks again into the telephone receiver, "Mr. Wilson, Mr. Nibs says he wants his own chauffeur because the London drivers are too reckless for him, they drive on the wrong side of the road and he doesn't trust them." There's another pause for a few seconds, "Yes Sir, I'll tell him, yes Sir, I'll give him your message. Good bye Mr. Wilson." Marcia hangs up the phone and turns toward Mr. Cuttleworth, "Mr. Wilson said he would make arrangements for all our passports, but we need to get photos of all of us first. He also said Mr.

Nibs to get all his shots and a certificate from the veterinarian showing him to be in good health, before he can leave for London, and he needs to be licensed."

"Licensed for what?" asks Cuttleworth.

"Mr. Wilson said he needed a cat's license."

"Why on earth would he need a license to be a cat? He's already a cat, he was born a cat and I'm inclined to believe he'll die a cat. So why on earth must he prove he's a cat by buying a license?"

"I don't know Mr. Cuttleworth, you'll have to ask Mr. Wilson about that."

"Shall I start packing Master Nibs' luggage?" asks Bentley.

"I think we had better talk to Mr. Wilson about this license first. I wonder if we too will need a license to prove we are humans."

"I think what Mr. Wilson was referring to is the same thing as a dog license." O'Harrah explains.

"A dog license? Now why would Nibs need a dog license? Nibs is not a dog, never was, Nibs is a cat."

"I didn't say he was a dog. What I said was a dog license is much like a cat license, in order to prove ownership he has to have a license."

"Nibs said no one owns him, he owns all of us and says if he has to wear a license around his neck, then all of us will have to wear one too if we want to continue keeping our jobs. Nibs said he is not going to be made into a fool by wearing a license by him self."

"Good gravy, do you mean to say that we will all be required to put collars around our necks like a dog?" asks Tracy in frustration.

"No Tracy, not like a dog, like a cat." Cuttleworth replies.

·   "Why I'll not wear a collar around my neck, why some one will think I'm some kind of kinky leather freak." O'Harrah says with concern.

"Nibs said once he gets to take off his collar the rest of us can take our collars off too.

"The Londoners already think Americans are strange, so we wearing collars probably won't have any affect on them. They will probably think it is a new American fad and maybe even copy us." Bentley says.

"If we all wear fancy jeweled collars people won't even notice. Why they will think it's just a new kind of necklace." Cuttleworth explains trying to calm the fears of Nibs' servants.

"I'm not going to wear any kind of jeweled collar! If I have to wear a collar, I'll wear one of those Indian necklaces that Indian warriors used to wear." O'Harrah says.

"Nibs said no, we must all wear cat collars if he has to wear one."

"It would have to be a very large necked cat that could wear a collar that would fit O'Harrah's fat neck." Marcia quips.

"There are large necked cats you know. Why some people keep pet lions and tigers in their homes and most of them have collars. We could just wear tiger collars."

Tracy explains.

"Well there you go. We will buy tiger and lion collars in keeping with Nibs' wishes by wearing collars like he does. Then I could have a metal shop stamp us all out a cat license with our names on them and we could all pretend we are cats. It might even be fun. We could pussy foot around. Be the cat's pajamas and even go out tom catting. Why once we get used to wearing them we will be the cat of the hour." Cuttleworth says cheerfully.

"Oh what I must put up with working for Master Nibs." sighs Bentley.

"Marcia, Nibs wants you to go down the hall and knock on Howard's door and tell him Nibs wants to see him right away."

"Yes Sir, Mr. Nibs, I'll leave right now." Marcia gets up and goes out the living room door that leads to the hall.

"Shouldn't we think about calling the crew in New York and telling them to prepare the yacht for a cruise to London?

Then notifying the pilot of his plane to fly us to New York." suggests O'Harrah.

"That is one reason Nibs wants Howard to come here. He wants him to take him in the limousine down town to shop for new collars for himself and a new outfit for me to wear in London. Then to arrange to have the car shipped by rail to New York to put a aboard the Cat Fish."

"Does the master want us buying new outfits too?" asks Bentley.

"No, Nibs said you can wear whatever pleases you. He just wants some fancy collars for himself since he is being required to have to wear a cat license. I still don't understand why he has to wear a cat license to prove he is a cat? Why just looking at him you can tell he is a cat."

"As far as a health certificate is concerned, I can arrange to get that from Dr. Highbill . He is a close friend of mine. However his rates are pretty expensive, but perhaps since he is a friend of mine you can get his services at cut rate." says Tracy.

"Oh Nibs doesn't want to get cut, he just wants a cat license, Tracy." Cuttleworth explains.

"I meant to save money."

"Nibs said he is rich now and he can well afford to pay for services needed and still does not want some doctor cutting in to him."

The door opens as Marcia and Howard enter as Marcia then speaks, "Here he is, Mr. Nibs"

Howard, the chauffeur is tall, lanky, around six foot, about twenty two years old. He has a long single braid in a pony tail going to his waist. He has a mustache and pointed goatee on his lean face. He wears an old fashion chauffeur's uniform; black knickers, high lace up black boots, white shirt, black bow tie, black chauffeur's jacket and black duckbill cap.

"Howard, Nibs wants you to go to London with us aboard his yacht the Cat Fish, and to drive him around in London, because he doesn't trust those London drivers."

"That's great! I know what Mr. Nibs is saying. I heard in London everybody drives on the wrong side of the street, but you won't catch me driving on the wrong side of the street, no Sir, I'll drive on the side of the street that we're supposed to drive on."

"But their steering wheels are also on the wrong side of the car." Marcia explains.

"Why can't Mr. Nibs bring his own limousine aboard his yacht?

He has a big enough cargo hold to have a limousine put aboard." Howard says.

"Nibs said that is a very good idea Howard. Then we'll have Nibs' limousine brought with us."

The telephone rings and Marcia answer it, "Hello, Mr. Wilson." There's a pause for a few seconds, "I'll tell him right away."

She hangs up the phone and says, "That was Mr. Wilson again, he said he would meet with you tonight here and go over all the legalities for all of us in order to be able to go to London and he said we will all need health certificates in order to get passports there."

"Nibs said no wonder those Londoners drive on the wrong side of the road, they are so afraid of germs they want visitors to have certificates and wear collars with licenses, therefore with loony customs like that he isn't a bit surprised of how they drive."

"They say Americans are bad drivers, at least we all don't drive on the wrong side of the road." Howard remarks.

"Will all of us be able to fit in Master Nibs' limousine though? There are seven of us you know, and Master Nib insists on his room." Bentley asks.

"Nibs said he must have his nurse in case he becomes ill from breathing the London pea soup fog, since he is allergic to pea soup, and he will need his body guard at all times by his side, plus his secretary to take notes for him of places to see, his lawyer in case he gets in a wreck with those terrible London drivers, and of course myself and Nibs because I am his guardian and Bentley his valet."

"The limousine he already has only carries ten persons in the back." Howard explains.

"Well then that ought to be big enough. Mr. Wilson will take up the space of two passengers, since he is so big and Nibs needs the room of two passengers in case he decides to stretch out and take a nap. Howard go and bring the car around the front entrance. Nibs and I want to go down town and do some shopping."

"Yes Sir. Does Mr. Nibs want me to fill the gas tank and bring extra gas cans along in the trunk before going to London?

I heard the gas prices overseas are five dollars a gallon." says Howard.

"That is five pounds, not five dollars." replies Bentley.

"Five pounds? That's outrageous! Why five pounds of one dollar bills would soon break Nibs. Yes, by all means fill up the tank here and go out after you drop us off downtown and buy as many gas cans you can that will fit in the trunk and fill them with gasoline. Five pounds of money! That's terrible!"

"Maybe it's only five pounds of pennies." suggests Marcia.

"Well even five pounds of pennies will soon mount up. Why we might end up paying hundreds of dollars for a mere gallon of gasoline. I have heard it is expensive to live in London, but this ridiculous. I'll bet people over there are far poorer that they are here paying those prices."

"Maybe we can't afford to go at all." says Bentley with a sigh.

"Nonsense, we may have to stay aboard the yacht we get there, but we will go none the less as Nibs has his heart set on it"

"Shouldn't I go downtown with you Mr. Cuttleworth to help Master Nibs pick out some nice collars?" suggests Bentley.

"That's a good idea, and while you're at it you can pick out a collar for yourself." Cuttleworth replies.

"Didn't you say we all needed collars?" Marcia asks.

"Nibs said that, not I and you can buy them on your own time before we leave. It will take us nearly a week to prepare to leave with getting our passports and all."

44

"I think all of this excitement is going to be hard on poor Mr. Nibs." says Tracy with concern.

"Nibs is far from being poor, he has well over thirty-five million yet after spending only fifteen million buying and remolding this and another building, buying the yacht, the limousine, the furnishings for this apartment and his winter home in Arizona. Plus he has assets of over three hundred billion. He is far, far from ever being poor again."

"Oh dear me how did he get all of that for only fifteen million?" asks Bentley as Mr. Cuttleworth replies, "He bought everything on the black market from the Republicans."

"What I meant was Mr. Nibs should take it easy."

"Nibs said now that he is rich he intends to always take it easy. Howard would you please go down stairs and get the car ready?"

"Yes Sir Mr. Cuttleworth, right away Sir." Howard goes to the door and opening it exits through the door.

"Well let's not sit around doing nothing; we all have to get ready for our trip."

Two weeks later aboard the yacht Cat Fish somewhere in the Atlantic Ocean in the main salon. The main salon is very large, over forty feet long, twenty-five feet wide by twenty feet high with four massive five tier crystal chandeliers suspended overhead.

The walls are done in rich red velvet wallpaper with white marble columns every ten feet and a large white marble fireplace setting against one wall. Elaborate Persian carpets lay upon the hardwood floors. Red velvet drapes with gold fringe borders the many massive windows overlooking the enclosed decks on both sides. The drapes are held back by gold braided robes. Expensive oil paintings by Monet, Eagle Ashcroft, Remington and Rubin in their gilded gold frames hang from the walls. The ceiling is vaulted with painted scenes of English gardens and cats at play. The furniture is red velvet upholstered Victorian and highly polished carved dark mahogany. There are Tiffany floor and table lamps everywhere. Spanish carved hardwood book cases line some walls with works by Voltaire, Hemingway, Eagle Ashcroft and Shakespeare.

Marble and bronze statues set on bookcases, tables and the floor along with coats of armor and carved crystal figurines. The room seems more befitting the grand hall of an expensive palace on land than on a ship at sea.

Nibs, Mr. Cuttleworth, O'Harrah, Marcia, Bentley, Mr. Wilson, Tracy, and Howard are all sitting around in the salon in various chairs and couches close together talking amongst themselves. Everyone is dressed in their usual attire as servants.

Cuttleworth wears a three piece light gray silk suit, white shirt, red tie. Wilson is still wearing his usual ill fitting Panama suit as O'Harrah wears his black suit.

It is evening, the sea is calm.

"Nibs said you all look so nice with your cat collars."

"I think we look ridiculous! The city dog and cat licensing bureau thought we were all touched in the head too when we insisted they issue us cat licenses." Wilson remarks with disgust in his words.

"Master Nibs would have not let us come along had we not gotten them" Bentley says.

"Mine looks like an expensive diamond necklace." Marcia remarks proudly.

"I am wondering if they are unhealthy to wear. It would seem they wouldn't let us breathe very well." Tracy says with concern.

"After I got mine all the girls were trying to date me, they thought I looked real macho." Howard says in good spirits.

"Yeah, well my old buddies on the police force practically laughed me out of town.

I'll never be able to live it down now."

"Well Nibs thinks you all look good and that's good enough for me."

"The worst part was when I asked to get a passport for Mr. Nibs, they flatly refused. They said they didn't issue passports to cats." Wilson says.

"Then how come Mr. Nibs has a passport?" asks Howard.

"Mr. Nibs arranged to send them on an all expense paid vacation for two weeks in Bermuda. Boy, you should have seen how fast Mr. Nibs got his passport after that." Wilson explains.

"They must have been Republicans," O'Harrah quips as Wilson replies, "Believe it or not they were Democrats."

"The photo studio thought Mr. Cuttleworth was daffy when he said he wanted a passport photo for Mr. Nibs." Howard injects.

"Yes, but after Mr. Nibs asked Mr. Cuttleworth to give the photographer a tip of a hundred dollar bill, he said' Mr. Nibs was his best customer." O'Harrah says joyfully.

"It's really strange how money can change a person's opinion of you." Marcia remarks.

"It's not really all that strange, people seem more healthy and happy when they receive money from strangers." Tracy says.

"Strange or not, when it comes to money everybody say's its normal to feel happy having it." Howard says.

"I do know that when Nibs and I had no money and we were getting by on social security we had few friends and no one wanted to help us, now since we are rich everybody wants to be our friend and help us."

"That's the way it goes, you're poor and friendless. You're rich and have more friends then you know what to do with." Wilson says. "Why after Mr. Nibs hired me on as his personal attorney my income is three times of what it was when I was in private practice, enabling me to live well. And I get more respect from people too, especially the ladies."

"You've kidding. Why the way you kept adding on charges to my bill when I wanted you to represent me in court over that eviction notice I'd say three or four cases like that a week would have made you a very rich man."

"It was standard procedure." Wilson responds.

"Standard procedure my foot. And by the way, what was the told tax anyway?"

"If I told you I would have had to charge you more money."

"Well Nibs said you had better answer right now or you may be back in private practice again when we get back home from London."

"It was just that, a tax to add if I told you."

"Your first name fits you well, you shyster."

"Actually it was my mother's maiden name. It's Irish. It actually means frugal."

"Irish my foot! Shyster not only does not mean frugal, but it means adding on charges here and there for things that don't even exist. Why a friend of mine, an honest attorney told me you were known to do this to everyone because you were lucky to get clients at all, so you bilked them out of their hard earned cash just to stay afloat." Cuttleworth says discerning.

"Dear me you mean to tell me there are actually honest attorneys?" quizzes Bentley.

"Then if that is so as you claim, why did Mr. Nibs hire me on as his personal attorney?"

"Because he said since you've such a shyster you might be able to talk a monkey out of giving up his banana in exchange for a worthless rock. And in which case should we ever get in a bad jam you might possibly get us back out with your shyster ways."

"I heard that when Mr. Nibs gets to London they might quarantine him for ten days." Says Howard.

"I don't think so, once Mr. Nibs asks Mr. Cuttleworth to slip a hundred dollar bill to each of the port officers, Mr. Nibs won't spending one hour in quarantine." explains Wilson.

"Won't they want a whole pound of money instead of a hundred dollar bill?" Marcia asks.

"Well, then I'll give them a pound of pennies, before we left I went down to the bank and had fifty thousand dollars changed into five pound sacks of pennies so we would have enough money while in London. It's all in the cargo hold along side of the limousine and the ten five gallon gas cans full of gasoline."

"I think it would be hard on our backs carrying around all of those sacks of pennies." Tracy remarks.

"Nibs had me buy a wheelbarrow to wheel the pennies around London with so we would always have spare change," explains Mr. Cuttleworth.

"If only Master Nibs had chosen the French Riviera instead we wouldn't have to carry so many pennies around with us." Bentley says.

"I certainly wasn't going to carry five pounds of dollar bills around with us."

"I heard the French were paid in francs." Marcia says.

"Then Mr. Nibs would have had to round up hundreds of persons with the name of Frank to trade for things. No, I think five pounds bags of pennies are better." says Howard.

"I tried talking Mr. Nibs in going to the Canary Islands instead. He could have found plenty of canaries to eat there." O'Harrah says.

"Nibs wanted to see London and after all he is the boss."

"Oh I do hope Master Nibs doesn't get sick wading through all that pea soup fog London is so famous for. You know how ill Master Nibs gets when he is exposed to pea soup." says Bentley with concerned strain in his voice.

"That's what worries me the most, Mr. Nibs becoming ill while he is in London from some foreign disease." Tracy says.

"I heard they call people in England "limeys", do you think it's because they all have Lyme's disease?" Howard asks.

"Oh I hope not, if Mr. Nibs becomes ill while in London it would ruin his vacation." Tracy says with great concern.

"Does Mr. Nibs plan on staying on his yacht while in London?" O'Harrah asks.

"No Mr. Nibs has made reservations for us all to stay at one of London's finest hotels while there; he has booked the entire top floor of the Banana Peel Arms Hotel overlooking London so we will all be together."

"Won't that be rather costly?" Bentley quizzes.

"It will slip right by Mr. Nibs," O'Harrah replies.

"Why do you think I had all that money changed into five pound bags of pennies?

Don't you worry Nibs has plenty of money."

"Heck, Mr. Nibs might even get to meet Puss and boots going to London Towne." Howard says.

"Puss and boots? What do you mean Puss and boots going to London Towne?" Cuttleworth asks.

"That's Puss in Boots, not Puss and boots. Puss was wearing boots and he went to London Towne wearing them." Wilson corrects.

"How come he was wearing boots, did he get bucked off his horse?" Howard asks.

"If Mr. Nibs met him I'll bet he would buy Puss a horse so he wouldn't have to walk to town." Wilson says.

"I thought Puss was a female?" Marcia quizzes.

"Puss was a female, Puss was a pussy cat." explains Wilson.

"Well we know she wasn't a pussy dog, so it stands to reason she was a pussy cat." O'Harrah remarks.

"I once knew a dog that was a pussy, he was afraid of his own shadow." Howard remarks.

"So why didn't you run his shadow off?" asks Marcia interested.

"I tried, but it kept coming back."

"You should have called the police."

"I did and they had a detective to shadow it and see where it went at night."

"So where did it go at night?"

"The detective never found out, it was just a dark mystery."

"Why are all of you calling London a town, I thought London was a city?" asks Tracy.

"It is a city, but when Puss in Boots went walking to London it was a town." Wilson replies.

"So what happened, did it suddenly become a city after Puss arrived? Was Puss a billionaire too, did she have a lot of buildings built all at once?" Howard asks.

"No Puss in Boot went to London a very long time ago when it was only a small town." Wilson replies.

"Then I doubt Mr. Nibs wants to know some old lady cat when he can meet some nice young London cat." Marcia says.

"Look, Puss in Boots was only a nursery rhyme to begin with!" explains Wilson.

"So is Mr. Nibs going on to Nursery Rhyme after he leaves London, and how much do you know about the place? Oh I hope he doesn't go there and become ill from some strange disease." Tracy says with great concern.

"I don't think Nibs is going to have time taking any side trips to see an old pussy cat."

"A nursery rhyme is a child's poem, not a town." Wilson explains.

"More n' likely Nibs won't have the time for listening to poems either."

"Just forget it." Wilson says shaking his head side to side.

"Well if Nibs want to go to Nursery Rhyme and listen to some poems then by golly we will go."

"Do you think they will require we have to have our passports stamped when we get to Nursery Rhyme?" asks Bentley.

"Wilson, how far is Nursery Rhyme from London, and I want you to find out if they require our passports stamped?" Cuttleworth inquires.

"And if it is cold we can stamp our feet too," says Marcia.

"We will need to know if they have any rare diseases there too." Tracy injects.

"Look nursery rhyme is not a place, it's a fairy tale, and it doesn't exist." says Wilson in frustration.

"Then how did Puss in boots manage to come from there if it doesn't exist?" Howard asks.

"Puss in Boots didn't exist either she was a figment of Mother Goose's imagination." Wilson explains.

"Figment sounds good, what other flavors of chewing gum do they have in London?" quizzes Marcia smacking her lips.

"If Puss in Boots never existed then how come Mother Goose was from Nursery Rhyme and how come Puss in Boots wasn't from there, just answer me that Mr. Big Shot Attorney?" Howard asks his arms folded over his chest and sitting straight up in his chair.

"Well maybe you ought to get hold of Mother Goose and see if she will introduce Puss in Boots to Nibs."

"Look for the last time Puss in Boots was made up for little children so they could learn poems and have entertainment; there is no such place as Nursery Rhyme and Mother Goose was a pen name of the author of these rhymes which were poems for children." Wilson tries to explain.

"Boy you are sure confused Mr. Wilson, first you say that some mother goose wasn't a goose at all, but the name of a pen and the rhymes are not rhymes at all, but poems, then you say Puss in Boots was only an entertainer and didn't go walking to London Towne after all." Howard says.

"Where did Nibs ever find this buffoon, in the dog pound?" Wilson says now with great disgust in his words.

"The young man means well, Nibs hired him after he learned he was homeless and out of a job."

"I can well understand how a buffoon like that would be out of a job. If he worked for me he would be out of a job again."

"I understand you were not much better yourself as an attorney. Mr. Wilson, when Mr. Nibs took you on as his personal private attorney, so you really have a nerve to talk about others." Marcia says defending Howard.

"At least I know how to separate fact from fiction and I know the difference between a nursery rhyme and reality!"

"I heard when you were on your own your career was a fantasy." Marcia quips.

"Now, now; let's not argue. Nibs doesn't like everyone arguing around him, he said he just wants peace and quite while he is on vacation."

"Yes, a piece of action and quite a bit of excitement if he has to put up with Howard and Marcia all the time." Wilson remarks.

"If we need any fish bait maybe Howard will volunteer, I hear tell fish go after strange lures." O'Harrah quips.

"So you look like a strange lure yourself O'Harrah." Howard says.

"Nibs said if any of you want to argue you can go out on the deck."

"Then you can see which of you makes better fish bait if the fish start jumping." Bentley quips.

"If anyone is going out on the deck they should dress warmly because it is cool out there and you could catch a cold." Tracy says.

"That's cod Tracy, not cold, who ever heard of cold fish?" Marcia corrects as Tracy replies, "You've a cold fish Marcia, and a cold is an illness.

51

"Just like Marcia," quips Wilson.

"I think I'll go out on the deck, because it's getting too stuffy in here." says Howard.

"Yeah Howard, you are pretty stuffy alright!" Wilson says.

"You Mr. Wilson are a stuffed shirt! I'm going to join Howard on the deck." Marcia says in a huff. "At least I don't go around misleading my employer in to telling him a lie about some cat that they claim exist then says they don't. No wonder your practice as an attorney was a flop."

Howard and Marcia go through the door out on the deck.

"She is right you know Wilson. Why Nibs said he doesn't know to believe you any more or not telling him that story about Puss in Boots. Why if Nibs looses trust in you he might let you go."

"Look Mr. Nibs, I am sorry for misleading you. I was just trying to explain about a famous character in a famous fairy tale and some how it just got out of hand and got to the point where every one misunderstood my intentions. I never meant or implied there was ever a character named Puss in Boots."

"Nibs said then never try to mislead him again or he'll fire you. You've forgiven for now."

"Thank you Mr. Nibs I'll do my best to make up for this."

"Bentley, Nibs wants to turn in for night, we will be in London in three more days and he will be very busy planning his schedule for when we arrive in London."

"Very well Sir, I will prepare Master Nibs for his bed. Will there be anything else?"

"No Bentley that will be all. When you have prepared Nibs for bed you can take the rest of the night off."

"Well I don't know about the rest of you, but I'm going to bed too." says Wilson.

Tracy, O'Harrah, and Mr. Wilson get up and exit the salon.

It was three days later. Nibs, Mr. Cuttleworth, Howard and Bentley are sitting in Nibs' swanky hotel suite's drawing room in the very ritzy Banana Peel Arms London Hotel.

It is done is a royal motif of Buckingham Palace complete with a marble fire place, ornate gold filigree furnishings and gilded gold framed paintings of the great masters. The rich marbled walls have yellow marble pillars set next to the walls. The floor is covered with a fine yellow and gold Persian rug with designs of banana peelings.

The high vaulted marble ceiling has a five tier gold and crystal chandelier on a gold chain hanging from its very center. The room is fit for a king.

"Is Master Nibs alright? He hasn't spoken a word in two hours." Bentley quizzes.

"He is still shaken up after that ride from his yacht to his hotel this morning in the limousine." replies Cuttleworth.

"I'm sorry Mr. Cuttleworth, I was trying to stay on the right side of the road, but those crazy London drivers kept driving on the wrong of the road." Howard says defensively.

"Nibs was never so terrified in his life. These London drivers must be the worst in the world. They just wouldn't drive on their own side of the road."

"They all honked their horns at us and shook their fists out their car windows as if we were in the wrong when it was they who were in the wrong." says Bentley.

"Even the buses were driving on the wrong side of the road.

And they had two story buses because there was so much traffic they didn't have anymore room for any more buses." says Cuttleworth.

"I thought drivers back home were bad; even the buses were driving on the wrong side of the road, you would think at least they would know better." Howard says.

"They must not be able to afford to buy a lot of buses either, because every one of them had a second story on it to make up the difference for the buses they didn't have." Bentley remarks.

"Nibs was so petrified that he didn't even enjoy the ride, when I called his attention to the tower bridge he was so scared he never even knew we drove over it."

"Did you notice that those fool Londoners built two castles just alike at each end of the bridge?" Howard quizzes.

"They probably ran out of room on the land. I heard that London is one of the largest cities in the world." Bentley suggests.

"After Nibs has rested some more we will take a tour of London and show him the sights, but first we will have to call the rest of our crew in here and see what schedules Nibs wants."

"So you're saying we are going to risk life and limb back out on the streets of London in Mr. Nibs limousine just so he can see the sights?" Howard asks.

"Exactly that is why Nibs wanted to come to London in the first place to see the sights."

"Do you want me to drive?" Howard asks.

"Well you are Nibs' chauffeur and that is your job to drive Nibs where ever he wants to go."

"But when he hired me on as his chauffeur he never mentioned anything about having to drive through a city full of crazy drivers who don't even stay on their side of the road."

"These Londoners are a mite backward you can barely understand what they are saying. They don't speak good English and their automobiles are pretty old fashion looking." Bentley remarks.

"Bentley, I want you to bring the rest of the crew here. Nibs is coming around now and wants to talk about his schedules for the day."

Bentley arises from his chair and heading for the door goes through the door and exits.

"Bentley is right, these Londoners better learn English because I couldn't understand a word they were saying. Then the hotel clerk kept trying to tell you that the hotel couldn't accept cats in the hotel, but I guess you told them Mr. Cuttleworth."

"I merely told them that Nibs had booked the whole top floor and it was he that was paying for it, since he was an American multi-billionaire."

"Did you hear that bell hop say that in America even the cats were rich and he thought if he moved to America he'd have a good chance of becoming rich if cats could become that wealthy."

"Well he could if he had a rich Londoner cousin who lived there, then died and left him a lot of money."

Suddenly the door leading out in the hall opens an Bentley returns followed by Marcia, Tracy, O'Harrah, and Mr. Wilson.

"Nibs wants to discuss his schedule for the day and wants everybody here."

"I had just returned from a stroll on the street below when Bentley knocked on my door. I'll tell you this much, it's a real mad house on the streets below. Every body in the city drives on the wrong side of the road, even the police, and the steering wheels are on the wrong side of the cars." Marcia says.

"Probably the manufacturer's fault is why they drive on the wrong side of the road.

The fools think since the steering wheel is on the wrong side of the car they are supposed to drive on the wrong side of the road."

Cuttleworth suggests.

"If you saw the police driving on the wrong side too then we are in big trouble." Howard says with concern.

"The police might figure rather then try arresting everybody for driving on the wrong side of the street they too must drive on the wrong side of the street to avoid an accident."

O'Harrah reasons.

"What they ought to do is force the manufacturers to recall all the cars and put the steering wheels on the right side of the cars. They are the ones to blame for the drivers who are driving on the wrong side of the road." Cuttleworth says.

"The steering wheels are already on the right side, they need to be on the wrong side so the drivers can drive on the right side." Wilson explains.

"What do you mean the steering wheels are on the right side and they need to be on the wrong side in order for the drivers to drive on the right side? That doesn't make a bit of sense." Cuttleworth tells Wilson looking at him while slowly shaking his head side to side in amazement.

"These Londoners don't make any sense either driving on the wrong side of the road." Howard says.

"All I know it is unhealthy for people, driving that way, why someone could get killed." Tracy says with a sigh.

"The streets run every which way and once we were even driving in Scotland before we could get to our hotel." Howard remarks.

"Scotland! I don't remember when we were driving in Scotland?" Cuttleworth quizzes.

"Well we weren't exactly driving in Scotland, but we drove right past it, because I remember the sign said Scotland Yard." Howard explains.

"It probably meant some Scotchman's yard." Marcia suggests.

"Well why on earth would some Scotchman put up a sign to let people know they were passing his yard?" Cuttleworth asks.

"He probably didn't want anyone thinking he was a crazy Londoner, so he let it be known he was from Scotland.' Wilson suggests.

"Yes that makes sense. I'd probably do the same thing to separate myself from the rest of the Londoners." Cuttleworth responds.

"I remember us passing that place, but he must have been a very rich Scotchman, because there was a large sky scraper setting next to the sign." Marcia says.

"He was probably a Lord or Earl of some kind." says Bentley.

"Maybe he was Lord Earl." suggests Howard.

"What if he's a prince?" Marcia asks.

"What would a Scottish prince be doing living in the middle of London in a skyscraper?" Cuttleworth questions.

"That's a good question, maybe he was exiled from Scotland, some times royalty screws up and they get exiled." Wilson suggests.

"If this Scottish prince were exiled for screwing up he should have never moved to London with the rest of the screw-ups." Bentley tries to suggest.

"Nibs said he agrees with you, Bentley, but Nibs said if this Scottish prince screwed up bad enough to be exiled that he couldn't pick a better place to move to than be with people like himself."

"Master Nibs is right, what better place could a screw-up exiled Scottish prince move to than a city full of screw-ups?" Bentley replies.

"We don't even know if he is a Scottish prince, you're all just assuming that." Wilson says discerningly.

"He might even be an exiled Scottish queen." Howard remarks.

"Scotland doesn't even have a queen, Scotland is part of England and England has only one queen." O'Harrah explains.

"If Scotland is part of England, then how could the prince from Scotland be exiled to England?" Marcia asks.

"Yes, Nibs want the answer to that one too."

"Well we haven't exactly established that he is an exiled Scottish prince, he could be an eccentric Scottish millionaire who prefers living in London rather than living in Scotland." Wilson suggests as an answer to Cuttleworth's question.

"He'd have to be eccentric to live in London." O'Harrah says.

"Nibs wants to take a nap for now, so you must all leave and come back in four hours to be ready for us all to go out to dinner."

Nibs, Mr. Cuttleworth, Bentley, O'Harrah, Marcia, Tracy, Howard, and Mr. Wilson are all sitting around again in Nibs drawing room in his hotel suite in formal attire ready to go to dinner in a London restaurant. It is near sundown as the sunlight is yellowed and dim in the room.

"Nibs has scheduled his program while in London and wants us all to be familiar with it. This evening we are first going to dinner, then on to see London's version of the play, "Cats."

Then tomorrow morning he wants to see Buckingham Palace and to make an appointment to see the queen. From there he wants to see the Tower of London and Piccadilly Circus before returning back here."

"I heard as a child from my mother that Puss in Boots went to see the queen in London Towne so is should be easy for a big billionaire like Mr. Nibs to get in to see her." Marcia injects matter of factually.

"I didn't know there was a circus in town?" quizzes Howard upon hearing Cuttleworth say Piccadilly Circus.

"We will have to be careful while at the circus because sometimes elephants have been known to go mad and trample people." Tracy warns.

"Especially after seeing Howard and Marcia it may be the worst elephant stampede on record just to get away from those two," quips Wilson.

"Ah the circus, I remember as a young lad growing up and the thrill of going to the circus." Bentley reminiscences.

"I've never been to a circus." Howard injects.

"I would have thought all circuses had monkeys. How come they wouldn't let you in Howard was it because they hadn't let you out of the zoo yet?" O'Harrah asks jokingly.

"No they weren't interested in wild monkeys like him self." Quips Wilson.

"You'll be lucky to get in Piccadilly Circus yourself Mr. Wilson; I heard they didn't need anymore clowns." Marcia remarks.

"Please, lets not argue, Nibs doesn't want us arguing before dinner because it upsets his appetite."

"Oh I hope Mr. Nibs doesn't become ill from all of our arguing. That would be terrible after he had his heart set on going to dinner and a play, to ruin his evening." Tracy says with concern.

"Master Nibs came all the way to London to have a good time and here we all are acting like a bunch of fighting dogs." Bentley says in defense of Nibs.

"Shouldn't that be fighting cats?" Howard quizzes.

"In your case Howard, it could mean fighting laughing hyenas." Wilson quips.

"If Howard is a hyena, then you must be one too because you said we could be laughing hyenas and you were arguing too Mr. Wilson." Marcia injects.

"Nibs said you've all acting like morons."

"In other words what Mr. Nibs is saying is we are all starting to act like Londoners." O'Harrah quips.

"It must be catching oh I do hope we don't get the same mental defects as the rest of the Londoners by staying in London too long." Tracy remarks.

"Master Nibs just said he doesn't want us arguing amongst ourselves anymore." Bentley tries explaining.

"Thank you, Bentley, Nibs said he wants to go to dinner, Howard, please go to the garage in the basement of the hotel and bring Nibs' limousine around front, and Bentley, bring Nibs' red velvet pillow so he can lay upon it while you carry him to his car."

It is the very swanky London restaurant of Phewy Smellz London's finest chef as Nibs, Mr.Cuttleworth, O'Harrah, Mr. Wilson, Howard, Tracy Bentley, and Marcia are all sitting around a large white linen covered table. Nibs is sitting before the table on a high chair that Cuttleworth found in the restaurant.

A waiter approaches. He is rather tall and lanky with dark brown hair parted to one side. He appears to be in his mid-twenties.

He is wearing the black uniform of a typical waiter as seen in most high class eateries in finer restaurants. He passes around the menus and says, "Good evening, I am Stanley the head waiter; I will gladly wait on you myself, however we have rules against animals being in this establishment. So the animal will have to leave."

"Howard, you heard the man, you'll have to leave." O'Harrah quips.

"Looks like you'll have to leave with me then, because you're a big ape." Howard remarks.

"I was referring to the cat."

"Nibs is no ordinary cat, he is our employer Sir." Cuttleworth corrects.

"I don't care if he is your father, the cat has to leave."

"I'll have you know that Nibs is a very rich cat from the United States worth billions."

"I don't care if he is the king of Arabia and worth trillions, he has to go."

"Master Nibs in not the king of Arabia, Mr. Cuttleworth never said he was the king of Arabia. You Londoners are not only backward, but deaf as well." Bentley says in defiance.

"That's telling him, Bentley." Howard injects.

"I am sorry Sir, but we have a strict policy about animals being in our establishment."

"Then what are you doing in it, Stanley?" Wilson quizzes jokingly.

"Obviously it is true what they say about the Americans all being a bunch of ignorant jokesters."

"Whom are you calling an ignorant jokester? I am Mr. Nibs' body guard and before I let you toss Mr. Nibs out I'll toss you out, you insulting twerp!" O'Harrah interacts.

"Look, you're making a scene if you don't remove the cat right now I'll call Mr. Harwood the manager."

"Why is he a cat too?" asks Marcia.

"No he is my boss and he does not tolerate any kind of animals in his establishment."

"If that is so how were you able to sneak in?" asks Wilson.

"Look I didn't make the rules, but I have to enforce them in order to keep my job."

"If that is the case then you need to quit because you are a skunk working in restaurant that does not allow your kind in it," says Wilson."

"Look I'll not argue with you Americans, unless you remove the cat I'll have to call the manager over to your table."

"If he is a dog just whistle and he will come," says Howard.

"But if he is a skunk we will all leave," says Marcia.

"Look I will not put up with your insults. Just remove your cat please."

"Young man, Nibs is a very wealthy individual who commands respect. Mr. Wilson there (Mr. Cuttleworth points his finger in the direction of Mr. Wilson) is Nibs' personal attorney and you young man better keep a civil tongue in your mouth or you're liable to be out of a job."

"Look, I didn't make the policy it is against the health codes of London to admit an animal into any eating establishment in London."

"You have a nerve quoting health codes when all of the London drivers drive on the wrong side of the road." Howard injects.

"Yes and they are endangering everyone's lives driving that way too." Tracy says.

"Mr. Nibs is in excellent health as he was checked by his veterinarian before he left the United States." Marcia says.

"It looks as if you all were checked by a veterinarian as well from the collars you are wearing."

"That was Master Nibs' idea he wanted all of us to wear cat collars if he had to wear one." Bentley explains.

"Did the veterinarian check you all for rabies shots too?

It seems you all need them, a talking cat, who ever heard of a talking cat?"

"Nibs talks to Mr. Cuttleworth through mental telepathy." Wilson explains.

"It sounds, more like a mental defect of Mr. Cuttleworth than mental telepathy."

"If you're the head waiter, I would hate to know what the foot waiter is like." Marcia remarks.

"Young man you are upsetting Master Nibs." Bentley says.

"I have a mind to punch you right in the nose you smart aleck young twerp!" O'Harrah says in anger.

"That does it I'm going to get the manager Mr. Harwood." Stanley turns on his heels and hurries away.

"The nerve of that brash young man, I'm going to recommend to the manager he be fired immediately." Wilson says.

"Nibs said he has never been so insulted in all his life since Mrs. Burnside was his landlady before he inherited all his money."

"Whatever happened to Mrs. Burnside?" O'Harrah quizzes.

"The last time I heard she was a manager of a flop house in skid row." Cuttleworth replies.

"A good position for the likes of her to be amongst bums of her ilk." responds Wilson.

Just then a tall well dressed man in a tuxedo of around forty five, rather tall and of medium built having a thin mustache, graying dark wavy hair and wearing a three piece pin-striped blue suit, blue tie against a white shirt approaches the table and says, "I am Mr. Harwood the manager of this restaurant. What is the trouble here? I understand you have an animal with you and you won't take him outside."

"He's your waiter, so you take him outside, he isn't with us." Howard quips.

Marcia and O'Harrah laugh.

"We don't allow animals in our establishment."

"So how come you're here then?" Marcia quips.

"Young lady, I'm not speaking to you."

"She is an employee of Nibs and she has the right to answer for

Nibs if she wants, and Mr. Harwood, you will not address Nibs as an animal. Nibs is a highly respected American billionaire with a vast real estate empire and we all are in the employment of him. And as his guardian I will not sit idly by while you insult him in this matter!"

"I've heard that you Americans were an odd lot, but that a cat is an American billionaire with a real estate empire is the most fantastic thing I have ever heard of."

"It is true! I am Mr. Nibs' attorney and Mr. Nibs is an American billionaire who owns vast real estate holdings including oil wells and several large businesses, including an empty clock store in Corona, New Mexico that tells time in five hundred time zones.

He also has a very large yacht at this present time tied up in the London harbor, as well as his own private jet, and a large winter home in Arizona with London Bridge in his back yard next to a bird bath the size of a lake."

"Quite matter of fact I must inform you that it is against the London health codes for an animal of any kind to be in an eating establishment."

"Nibs has enough money to buy this place, fire you and turn it into a restaurant for cats only. So you better act more civilized in Nibs presence or you might find yourself out of a manager's job."

"Look , I'm not trying to be a hard person to get along with, that's just the health codes the city of London has established for all eateries, perhaps we can fix a special free meal you can bring to your cat to where ever you are staying to make up for the inconvenience."

"We don't have an inconvenience! You are the inconvenience!

We are only here to order dinner, but you seen to want to cause us trouble." Cuttleworth explains his voice rising in anger.

"Look you may all stay and have dinner, but the cat can't stay.

I am sorry but you are going to have take the cat outside."

"You don't address Mr. Nibs as "THE CAT," I'm his body guard and if you make another remark like that I'm going to punch you in your big fat nose!"

"Please calm yourself Sir. I apologize in calling your Mr. Nibs a cat. Will you kindly remove Mr. Nibs from the premises now?"

"No we will not remove Nibs from the premises now or any other time until he has eaten his dinner first."

"I see, so you are going to be difficult are you?"

"It is you Sir whom is being difficult." Cuttleworth says.

"This is so bad on Mr. Nibs' health with all this excitement." Tracy says with concern.

"Master Nibs is being treated in such a shoddy way unbecoming an individual of his feline stature. It is a travesty of justice." Bentley says.

"It is unconstitutional. Every American regardless who they are ought be treated equal." Howard fumes.

"You're not in America now Sir, this is Great Britain, you are in her Majesty's country."

"Ha, ha. What's so great about Britain with idiots like you running a London restaurant?" O'Harrah laughs.

"O'Harrah is right, Britain isn't so great. America is greater.

In fact we are from great America." Howard injects.

"Then perhaps you should go back there because in London we do not allow cats whether they are Mr. Nibs or any other cat to be in an eating establishment."

"If you don't serve Nibs and continue in this uncivilized matter, I am going to ask O'Harrah to throw you out of your own restaurant."

"I see you can't be reasoned with, so unless you all leave right now I am going to call the police and have you all forcefully removed including that filthy animal." Says Harwood starting toward Nibs with his out stretched arm threatening to grab him by the back of the neck as O'Harrah quickly rises and punches Mr. Harwood in the nose knocking him backward against another patron's table. He falls knocking the table over and its patrons to the floor. Stanley who is standing a way off now comes to Mr. Harwood's rescue and takes a swing at O'Harrah. Howard turns on Stanley and punches him in the stomach. Marcia kicks him in the shins. Then a restaurant patron comes to the rescue of Stanley and Mr. Harwood taking a swing at Howard. Mr. Cuttleworth hits him over the head with a menu as Tracy socks him in the jowl. Then O'Harrah punches both Stanley and the patron in the jowl. Nibs springs from his seat and lands in the middle of a patron's table dumping hot gravy on them and then jumping to another table in the melee as other patrons scream and yell as he jumps on top of a stately matron's head forcing her face to fall forward in the banana pie she is eating, then as he leaps away her blond wig falls to the floor revealing her head is bald underneath. Then tables over turn one by one as other patrons join the melee. Some one screams, "Call the police!"

It's a London jail cell; it is a large pen like cell with both the women and the men of Nibs' staff put in together. There are no other prisoners in with them. It seems to be a separate jail than the regular jail. Perhaps part of a police station even. There are cots hanging from chains against the walls where some of Nibs' staff sit while others stand or lean against the bars. Only Nibs is not with them.

"O'Harrah, you shouldn't have lost your temper and hit Mr. Harwood then you had to hit Stanley as well." Cuttleworth says.

"But you said I was to protect Mr. Nibs."

"I hadn't given you the order to fight."

"But he called Mr. Nibs a filthy animal."

"Mr. Nibs isn't a filthy animal, he had a bath before leaving for the restaurant. In fact he is always washing himself." Tracy says.

"Mr. Harwood had no right calling Mr. Nibs a filthy animal anyway." Marcia says.

"Now he will be a filthy animal since the police took him to the dog pound until we have to go to trial." says Bentley.

"If Mr. Nibs heard you call him a filthy animal he would probably leave you in London when he goes back home." Howard remarks.

"I take that back, a filthy cat then."

"We are in one heck of a mess now, here we are in a foreign country in some third world jail and Mr. Nibs is in the dog pound and alone." Howard says.

"Don't they have other cats there to keep him company?" Marcia asks.

"That's not the point, he isn't with the people he is familiar with, and we have to prepare our defense." Wilson says.

"That's your job, that's what Nibs hired you for just in case something like this was to happen."

"Mr. Nibs will probably come down sick from some unknown illness while in the pound." Tracy says with concern.

"Dear Master Nibs, I feel so sorry for him, he is without a valet to prepare his bed and lay out his collars." Bentley says with a sigh.

"We'll all be lucky to keep our jobs after this thing is over with." Cuttleworth remarks.

"I'll probably be the first one he fires for losing my temper and hitting those idiots." O'Harrah says.

"Well you were just doing you job. You were hired to guard Nibs but you lacked judgment. You were only to attack if Nibs' life was in danger or if they had laid a hand on him from the restaurant."

"That Mr. Harwood didn't have any right calling Mr. Nibs a filthy animal after Tracy said he had taken a bath before coming to the restaurant." Howard says.

"Howard shut up, this is no time to be making jokes, and can't you see how much trouble we are in?" Wilson asks more as a statement than a question.

"Do you think we will all go to prison?" Marcia asks.

"I doubt that, but O'Harrah might." Wilson replies.

"Not if you do your job right he won't." Cuttleworth says.

"You forget we are in England, not America. The laws and courts are a lot different over here than in the United States." Wilson says.

"These third world countries I heard don't have any justice, if you break their laws I heard they just take you out and shoot you." Marcia tries to explain. "I heard in these backward countries they just take you and execute you without the benefit of a trial."

"That's not so Marcia. This is England they are more civilized than that." Wilson explains.

"Oh yeah, then how come they tried throwing Mr. Nibs out of the restaurant then?" Howard asks.

"Yes, how come they wanted to throw Master Nibs out of the restaurant if they are so civilized?" Bentley asks.

"We are in a foreign country with their own set of laws and perhaps prestige and money doesn't man anything to them." Wilson suggests.

"Maybe with all their royalty and wealth I suppose prestige and wealth are considered common place here." O'Harrah says.

"I wonder what my Nibs is thinking at this time?"

"I'll bet he is thinking he wished he had not come to London." Howard suggests.

"I think we would have all been better off had Mr. Nibs chosen to go to Paris instead." Marcia says.

"I tried talking him into going to Paris, but he was stead fast in wanting to come to London."

"I'll bet Master Nibs wished he had listened to you now." Bentley injects.

"Why did the jailer take our collars away from us, did they think we were going to hang ourselves with them?" Howard asks.

"They always take your jewelry away from you when you are put in jail. They'll be returned to us after we go to trial." O'Harrah replies.

"Do you think they took Mr. Nibs collar too?" Marcia asks.

"I doubt that, they let cats keep their jewelry while incarcerated."

Wilson explains.

"How come we are in jail and Mr. Nibs gets incarcerated?" Howard asks.

"Mr. Nibs has prestige, that's why." Marcia replies.

"Incarcerated means to be locked up." Wilson explains.

"Fancy lawyer talk." Howard remarks.

"This is the first time in Nibs' life since he was a kitten nearly fourteen years ago that he and I have been separated."

"Oh he must be in mental torment." Tracy says sadly.

"Well they had better not be torturing him or so help me when I get out of here I'll go down to the pound and beat the living daylights out of everybody working there." O'Harrah says his fists clenching and unclenching.

"No you won't O'Harrah, that's how we got into this mess in the first place. If you had only kept your wits about you Nibs would have bribed Harwood and we could have gone on and had dinner there. But no, you lost your temper."

"So now I'm going to get all of the blame for this incident."

"Well it is true you lost your head and hit the manager and the head waiter. Mr. Nibs would have bought off the manager if you had just waited." Wilson says.

"Heck, Mr. Nibs could have bought the whole restaurant and had Stanley and Mr. Harwood fired for that matter." Howard remarks.

"Why he could have bought the whole city of London and had all the Londoners fired." Marcia says.

"He isn't that rich." Cuttleworth says.

"It's a good thing I am Mr. Nibs' lawyer because if anything he will at least get a good American attorney to represent him."

"If Mr. Wilson fails, Mr. Nibs' money can bribe the judge to let us all go." Howard says.

"Yes, that is true, money talks." Cuttleworth says.

"What does it say when it talks?" asks Marcia.

"That Marcia is an idiot." replies O'Harrah.

"Then the judge could attach bribery to Master Nibs' charges too." says Bentley..

"No country on earth will charge a cat for bribery." explains Wilson.

"If that is the case, then how could they even have had Mr. Nibs arrested and put in jail?" Howard asks.

"He was not put in jail he was put in the pound for his own protection while we were put in jail." Wilson replies.

"That's my job protecting Mr. Nibs." O'Harrah says.

"Well you can't protect him since you got yourself in hot water for punching out Harwood and his head waiter." Cuttleworth injects.

"But why were the rest of us arrested? We hadn't done anything." quizzes Marcia.

"You all took part in the fight." Cuttleworth replies.

"Only after O'Harrah started it and we had to defend him since he works for Mr. Nibs." Marcia replies.

"We were accomplices." Wilson says.

"I'm not an accomplice. I am an American partner in crime." Marcia responds.

"Accomplices means partners in crime." Wilson explains.

"We weren't O'Harrah's partners we are just employees of Mr. Nibs." Howard says.

"As employees of Mr. Nibs we are all considered partners in crime since it was Mr. Nibs' employee, O'Harrah that committed the crime of battery." Wilson explains.

"I didn't know it was against the law in England to own a battery?" Marcia quizzes.

"Battery means striking someone." Wilson explains.

"So what's that little black box under the hood called that starts Mr. Nibs' car up, a striker?" Howard asks.

"Where did you ever get your brains Boy, in a joke shop?" Wilson asks in disgust.

"No as a matter of fact when Howard was born God just gave out the last brain to the person born prior to him, so when he got to Howard he was fresh out of human brains, so he gave him a duck's brain instead." quips O'Harrah.

"Quarreling amongst ourselves isn't going to solve any problems. We have to get our defense together and decide what we're going to say in court." Cuttleworth says his chin resting on the palm of his right arm as he sits on the edge of his cot.

"I have my own defense, I'll plead insanity." Marcia says.

"If you keep hanging out with Howard you won't need to convince anyone you're insane, it'll become an established fact." O'Harrah quips.

"I'll do the talking when we get in the courtroom, but I'll insist that Mr. Nibs be there as a witness to the ill treatment that Harwood and Stanley gave him." Wilson states.

"What if the judge tries barring Nibs from appearing in his court?"

Cuttleworth quizzes.

"These English are a lot different than Americans, their judges are said to all wear powdered wigs and are so hard to understand that I believe they wouldn't refuse my request." Wilson replies.

"Why do they wear powdered wigs?" Marcia asks.

"Because they are English and the English are odd." Wilson explains.

"That's for sure, they drive on the wrong side of the road, they can't even speak English right and now you tell us that their judges wear powdered wigs; does their queen also wear the pants in the family too?" Howard asks.

"In a sense yes, she is the ruler of this country." Wilson replies.

"Don't the judges know putting too much powder in their hair can cause baldness?" Tracy asks.

"Is that what you do Mr. Wilson, put too much powder in your hair? You don't seem to have much." O'Harrah jokingly asks.

"Then you must have been born with powder on your brains, because you don't seem to have any." Wilson quips back.

"Please, please lets not argue amongst ourselves, we have bigger things to worry about than who wears a lot of powder." Cuttleworth says.

"I wear a lot of powder on my face sometimes." Marcia says.

"That explains why you are sometimes so faceless." O'Harrah quips.

"Just what do you mean by that remark?" Marcia asks.

"Well for one thing you're always sticking up for that lame brain, Howard." O'Harrah replies as a matter of fact.

"Everybody is always picking on him and if you really knew him you'd find out he is a warm and caring person." Marcia defends Howard.

"Marcia is right, Nibs said the same thing. O'Harrah if you continue insulting Nib's employees I will report you to him when I see him again."

"I am sorry Mr. Cuttleworth, but if Mr. Nibs didn't have so many flakes in his employment I wouldn't insult them so much."

"Well it isn't your job to judge whether their flakes or not, Nibs hired them and it is up to Nibs if he wants to keep them whether they are flakes or not."

"Do you all realize how late it is getting? I heard Big Ben toll twelve times quite some time ago. It must be near one o'clock in the morning by now." Bentley remarks trying to change the heated subject.

"Bentley is right, we all need to turn in for the night in order to ready for court in the morning." Wilson says.

"I sure hope there aren't any bed bugs in here." Marcia says.

"Did you know bed bugs can cause you to be ill?" Tracy quizzes everyone.

"I wonder why they put the women in with the men?" Howard asks.

"I asked the jailers about that and they told me they don't usually put the men and women together, but since we were American tourist who were all going to court in the morning anyway, that we might as well stay together." Wilson explains.

"I think it is disgusting these English putting us all in the same cell together, I need my privacy!" exclaims Marcia.

"The English aren't a very modest race anyway otherwise their judges wouldn't go around in public wearing powdered wigs like a bunch of old women." O'Harrah says.

"Why would men want to look like an old women?" asks Howard.

"Because they never would get away with trying to looking like young women." O'Harrah replies.

"Let's all turn in for the night and cut the small talk." says Cuttleworth.

Mr.Cuttleworth, Mr. Wilson, Bentley, O'Harrah, Howard, Tracy, and Marcia are all assembled at a table in the London Municipal Court before Magistrate Judge Phillip Winston, a large man appearing to be in his late fifties. He wears small gold rimmed square glasses on his clean shaven face, a white powdered wig and black judge's smock makes him appear as if he just stepped out of the eighteenth century.

The prosecutor, Lord Sniff Snuff is a tall lanky man in his early forties with a handle bar mustache, he also wears a white powered wig and old fashion clothes from the late eighteenth century England. In fact both he and the judge seem out of place as if they were actors playing scenes from a Hollywood movie. The courtroom its self is large with dark paneled wood walls, two overhead globes suspended on chains hang from the tall plain ceiling are the lights for the courtroom. The benches look as if they had been borrowed from a church. The floor is covered in a dark brown carpet. Four tall windows framed by dark brown cotton drapes look out on the city of London. Above and behind the judge's high bench are two framed photographs, one of the queen of England and the other it's prime minister. And on one side of the judge's bench is the flag of Great Britain. On the other is the flag for the city of London. Lord Snuff opens an old fashion fourteenth century scroll as he exclaims while standing in front of the judge's bench facing those present in the courtroom, Wilson, O'Harrah and Cuttleworth sitting before a dark colored hardwood table to the left of the judge's bench, the other table of the same type of wood, but to the right of the judge's bench, empty, "Hear ye, hear ye!   This court is now in session, his Lordship the honorable Phillip Stephan Everly Ralph Richard Samuel Pickle Bert Winston is presiding."

The judge bangs his gavel as he announces, "I am his Lordship the honorable Phillip Stephan Everly Ralph Richard Samuel Pickle Bert Winston, Magistrate and Municipal judge for the city of London."

Howard whispers to Marcia sitting next to him in the front spectator's row, "Boy these English sure go in for long drawn out titles and middle names don't they?"

"Which one of you is called O'Harrah?" The judge asks.

O'Harrah raises his arm and say's "I am your Honor."

"That's your Lordship, O'Harrah." Lord Snuff corrects.

"That's alright, you need not call me your Lordship, and I'm just a plain old body guard for Mr. Nibs."

"I was referring to the judge."

"You English really go in for your titles, don't you, is the judge a knight too?"

Howard whispers to Marcia, "He looks more like a bad day."

"His Lordship is not a knight; he is a judge only. We call our judges lords."

Howard again whispers to Marcia, "They ought to call them ladies with their powdered wigs"

"We call our judges, your Honor in America."

"Well you Americans are a bit balmy anyway." Lord Snuff remarks to O'Harrah.

"Mr. O'Harrah do you have a first name?" asks the judge.
"Yes I have a first name your Honor."

"I am your lordship to you and what is your first name?"
"Can we just dispense with the fancy titles and let us call you judge instead?"

"You Americans are incorrigible! You will call me your Lordship the same as everyone else."

"Your Honor, I represent all of Nibs' employees and O'Harrah is an employee of Nibs." injects Wilson.

"Just who are you Sir and who is Nibs?' asks the judge.

"I am Mr. S. L. Wilson, Nibs' attorney, and Nibs is O'Harrah's employer."

"Who is Nibs?"

"A wealthy American cat and our employer."

"A wealthy American cat you say, a cat?"

"That's what I said, a cat."

"I never in my whole life ever heard of such a tale; you Americans indeed are a strange lot."

Howard whispers again to Marcia, "He thinks we Americans are a strange lot.

These stupid English are so backward they don't know which side of the road to drive on and that is a strange lot."

"It is true we all work for a cat." injects O'Harrah.

"Where is this cat right now?"

"I was going to ask you Judge if you could have Mr. Nibs taken out of the pound where he is being held and brought here as a witness as to why we are all here." Wilson replies.

"Bring a cat in my courtroom? This is unheard of to have a cat brought into my courtroom. How do you propose to make this cat a witness?"

"Mr. Cuttleworth is his guardian and interpreter." Wilson replies.

"You mean to tell me that Mr. Cuttleworth can understand a cat's language?"

"Yes your Honor, he can."

"Which one of you is Mr. Cuttleworth?"

Mr. Cuttleworth raises his hand "I am Sir."

"Just how are you able to understand this cat?

"Years ago when I first got Nibs he just meowed like any other cat and like any other cat I couldn't understand what he was saying. Then one cold night I became ill and didn't know what was wrong with me. Nibs got up next to me on the couch and spoke to me just like you are now, but it was coming into my thoughts.

At first I thought I was losing my mind, but then he told me to go to the herb store the next day and ask for a certain herb and I'd be cured. Well I was so ill already I didn't think I'd make it through the night, but Nibs told me not to worry, I'd live long enough to make it to the herb store, home again, and long enough to eat the herb to cure me."

"What a strange tale, you actually heard this cat talking to you as I am talking to you now?"

"Well no Sir, he was speaking English so I could understand him."

"What language do you think I am speaking?"

"I haven't got the faintest idea, but I know it isn't English because I can understand English and I can barely understand you."

"I am speaking the King's English."

"Why can't you speak your own English so Mr. Cuttleworth can understand you? Let the King speak for himself." Wilson quips.

"This is what everybody in England speaks, but go on Mr. Cuttleworth, so what happened?"

"Well I made it through the night and the next day I was still very ill, but I managed to make my way to the herb shop and I bought the herb Nibs told me to get then I ate it when I got home and that evening I was fine again."

"It sounds almost unbelievable, but how do you know it was Nibs speaking to you and not some thought conjured up in the back of your mind about some long forgotten thought of that herb?"

"I thought of that too, so to be sure Nibs was speaking to me I asked him things that only he could possibly know and he told me the answers, then I checked the answers out for myself and he was telling the truth."

"I must have this cat brought to my court room and ask him some questions my self that I only I know and if can answer them right I'll believe you and let him be a witness. Lord Sniff Snuff, go out and tell the bailiff to notify the pound that I give my order to have Mr. Cuttleworth's cat brought here to my court room."

"Yes your Lordship." Lord Snuff leaves the court room through the door.

"How did he come about getting the name Nibs?"

"When I was a little boy my father told me he had kitten named Nibs whom he loved very much, but where he lived they didn't allow pets, so his father made him give up his cat and he missed it so much he was unhappy from then on as a child. So I decided in memory of my dear old dad's pet kitten Nibs after I found this poor little homeless skinny kitten one cold winter night wandering in an alley and brought him home I'd name him Nibs. My father named his kitten Nibs because when he found it, it was just a little nib of fur. And when I found Nibs he too was just a little nib of fur. So instead of naming him Nib, I preferred Nibs like my own father's cat."

Judge Winston has tears in his eyes as he speaks to Mr. Cuttleworth, "That's a soul rendering tale, please go on, did Nibs ever tell you how he learned English and how he learned to speak?"

"I asked him the same thing and he said it just happened to him one day when he woke up; that suddenly he could understand English and found he could talk to me through my thoughts even though I could not speak to him the same way."

"I never heard such a strange story. An English speaking cat who can converse with someone through their thoughts. Can anyone else hear Nibs speaking through their thoughts? Has Nibs ever told you anyone else can hear him through their thoughts?"

"No, he never has told me anyone else can hear him, but then Nibs is my cat and that could be the reason."

"So how did Nibs come to be so wealthy?"

"Well I had a cousin I had forgotten about for several years, Nibs had saved his company once from going broke by telling him some very good financial advice. So when he died he willed his entire estate to Nibs and made me his executer and guardian."

"I could use a cat like that in helping me with my own finances." "Nibs doesn't work for anyone, he doesn't have to, and he's rich. In fact we all work for him."

"I mean I could use his advice."

"That's the reason we are all here in your courtroom and why O'Harrah had been charged with battery for defending Mr. Nibs against those bullies Harwood and Stanley who were about to bodily throw Mr. Nibs out of their restaurant because he was a cat." Wilson explains. "I'll hear Mr. Harwood and Stanley's testimony, otherwise its hearsay."

Just then the door of the court room opens and Lord Snuff comes in holding Nibs in his arms which he hands over to Mr. Cuttleworth, Nibs seems very happy to see his owner.

"Is this Nibs?" asks the judge.

"Yes your Honor."

"The pound couldn't have been very far away or Mr. Nibs wouldn't have been brought here this quickly." says Wilson.

"The pound is across the street from the jail and court." replies Judge Winston.

"Oh my, dear Nibs wasn't very far away."

"If everyone will raise their right hand and paw Lord Snuff will swear you all in and we can begin."

"You mean you're going to let Nibs be a witness without proving that he can really speak

to Mr. Cuttleworth?" Wilson asks the judge.

"No, after he is sworn in with the rest of you I am going to give him some questions that only he can answer and if he gives the right answers he can be a witness."

"Okay everybody raise their right hand and paw and repeat after me…"

Mr. Cuttleworth interrupts Lord Snuff, "But Nibs can't raise his paw, and I'll have to take the oath for him."

"Oh alright, very well, everybody repeat after me; I pledge to tell the truth, the whole truth, nothing but the truth so help me God." Everybody together repeats the oath.

"Nibs won't repeat the oath because it has God in the end and he does not believe in God. He believes cat created everything. He said if you will replace God with cat he'll take the oath." Cuttleworth explains.

"Your Lordship, what is your advice in this matter?" Lord Snuff asks.

"This is highly irregular and unheard of, but I'll make an exception this time because I have to find out for myself how intelligent this cat is. Lord Snuff give the oath again to Nibs, but replace God with cat."

"Yes your Lordship. Mr. Cuttleworth please raise your right hand again for Nibs and have him repeat the oath. I swear to tell the truth the whole truth and nothing but the truth so help me cat. Did he agree this time?"

"He did. He repeated every word." Cuttleworth replies.

"I never heard a peep out of him." says the judge.

"Of course not your Honor. That is because he talks to me through my thoughts as I formally explained to you."

"Very well I'll except that for now. O'Harrah you never did tell me your first name."

"It's McGinnery, your Honor."

"McGinnery? I had a great uncle from Scotland with the first name of McGinnery. Who named you thus?"

"My mother."

"Where was your mother from?"

"Scotland."

"What was her maiden name?"

"McGregor."

"Was her father O'Hanna O'Boy McCall O'Reilly McGregor?"

"Why yes it was."

"Her father and my father are cousins. That makes us cousins also."

"Then you should excuse yourself from this case your Lordship if the defendant is related to you." interrupts Lord Snuff.

"No, I'll not excuse myself, I want to hear this case and see if Nibs can really speak and understand English."

"I protest!" exclaims Lord Snuff.

"You can protest all you want Lord Sniff Snuff, but I'll not excuse myself from this case, so you can sniff that up your nose Lord Sniff Snuff. Mr. Cuttleworth I wish to ask Nibs what it looked like inside of the pound where he stayed last night. Who was in charge and what color were the walls inside the pound?"

"Nibs said a Mr. Patrick Matrick Hatrick Kinney Hinney was in charge, that it was a real dark cold dreary stinky place that smelt of skunks, the walls were dark and light sickening green, and the food was left over scraps from a restaurant, probably the same one they would not serve him in"

"That's incredible! He is exactly right, I believe you now."

"In that case I suppose if his lordship excepts your cat Nibs as having the intelligence to speak through Mr. Cuttleworth, he may testify." Lord Snuff says.

"Thank you your Lordship." says Cuttleworth.

"How come you are calling him lordship and not me?" asks Judge Winston.

"Because he is a lord and you're not."

"Well if he is my cousin then I'll address him as his lordship, we cousins have to stick together."

"By Jove old boy, you and I are going to get along just fine."

"Lord Sniff Snuff please ask the plaintiffs to come in." orders the judge.

Lord Snuff goes out and brings Mr. Harwood and Stanley into the courtroom.

"Lord Sniff Snuff will you swear in the plaintiffs?"

"Will the plaintiffs raise their right hands and repeat after me, I swear to tell the truth, the whole truth, and nothing but the truth so help me God?" Harwood and Stanley repeat the oath after Lord Snuff.

"Which one is Hardwood?" the judge asks.

Harwood now sitting before the right side table stands and says, "I am your Lordship."

"Please give your full name before the court." orders the judge.

"William Albert James Edward Victor Maurice Charles George John Harwood, your Lordship."

Howard whispers to Marcia, "No wonder he prefers to be called Harwood. I'd hate to have to call him to dinner, dinner would be over by the time I finished calling his name."

"Mr. Harwood please give your version of what happened last night in your restaurant?"

"Certainly your Lordship, the people sitting at that table over there (pointing to the table with Nibs' employees) were in my restaurant. Stanley the head waiter was serving them personally. When Stanley saw they had a cat with them he asked them to remove the cat…"

Judge Winston interrupts, "Mr. Harwood, were you there at the time that Stanley asked them to remove Nibs?"

"No your Lordship."

"Then that is hearsay. Just tell me what you your self heard."

"Stanley came and got me in my office and told me that the Americans sitting at a table would not remove the cat from the restaurant and that one gentleman had threatened him with bodily harm if he tried to forcibly have the cat removed. So I approached the table of the Americans and told them they would have to remove the cat, they refused and that big fat old guy over there (pointing to O'Harrah) punched me in the nose and knocked me down. Then he punched Stanley in the nose too and then the cat's owner and his friends got in on the melee then someone called the police and the police came and arrested them."

"Do you have a witness?"

"Yes your Lordship, my head waiter Stanley saw it all."

"Stanley will you stand and state your full name for the court?"

"Stanley Louis Mathew Luke Paul Robert Samuel Stephan Franklin Wishingtonhampton, your Lordship."

Howard again whisper to Marcia, "Now we know why he prefers to be called Stanley."

"Please Stanley give the court your version."

"I introduced myself to the Americans sitting there (pointing in the direction of Nibs employees) and told them I was their waiter. Then I discovered the cat there (pointing toward Nibs) and asked them to remove the animal. They refused and that older gentleman there, (pointing to Mr. Cuttleworth) threatened to have that big fat guy (pointing to O'Harrah) punch me if I tried to forcibly have the cat removed."

"Then what happened?"

"Then your Lordship, I went to see Mr. Harwood and told him, he came back with me and tried reasoning with them, but the big fat guy punched Mr. Harwood in the nose and then punched me in the nose too. Then everyone at their table got in the fight"

"Do you have anymore witnesses?"

"No your Lordship, we don't. I tried to locate some of the patrons that witnessed everything that day, but could not and in the excitement I forgot to get their names."

"Your Lordship, we are ready to hear the defendant."

"O'Harrah you may stand and tell your side of the story." says Judge Winston.

O'Harrah rises from the table he is sitting before as he speaks,

"Well most of what Mr. Harwood and Stanley say is true, but I was hired as Mr. Nibs' body guard; now when Mr. Harwood called my employer Mr. Nibs a filthy animal and threatened to have him forcibly thrown out of the restaurant I acted quickly to protect Mr. Nibs from harm by hitting the would be attacker, then Stanley there (pointing to Stanley) took a swing at me and I had to deck him too. As for the rest of Mr. Nibs employees they came to his defense also because they were protecting their employer as well "

"Do you have any witnesses?"

"Yes your Lordship, I do."

"You may call your first witness."

"I call Mr. Nibs to the stand."

"I protest, a cat can't be a witness." says Harwood.

"Mr. Nibs has been sworn in and I will decide who shall or shall not be a witness in my court room. Do I make myself clear, Mr. Harwood?"

"Yes your Lordship."

"Mr. Nibs, you may give your testimony now."

"Nibs said…," (Mr. Harwood cuts him off), "How can you let some one else speak for the witness?"

"Mr. Cuttleworth is Mr. Nibs' interpreter. Now shut up Mr. Harwood and don't interrupt again or I'll have you forcibly removed!"

"Nibs said he was in danger of his life and felt himself in harm's way and felt if O'Harrah and the others had not acted when they did, he might not be alive to be here to testify today. He said O'Harrah's job was to protect him against harm and he feels justified that O'Harrah acted in his best interest as well as his other employees."

"Is that all?"

"Yes your Lordship."

"O'Harrah, call your next witness."

"I call Mr. Cuttleworth to the stand."

Before Mr. Cuttleworth can get up Lord Snuff arises and approaches the Judge, "Your Lordship, Mr. Harwood and Stanley have decided to drop the charges of battery against the defendant."

"Is that so Mr. Harwood and Stanley?"

"Yes your Lordship. In the best interest of American-British relations we have decided to drop all charges against the defendants." Harwood replies.

"Stanley, do you agree with Mr. Harwood?"

"Yes your Lordship."

"I have decided to make my own ruling regardless. First of all I want to say that Mr. Harwood and Stanley acted uncouth and ungentlemanly, so I am ordering them to not only let Mr. Nibs and his employees back in their restaurant to eat, but in addition they will also be required to give them the best table and house service. Let them order as much as they want and do not charge them any money whatsoever. If they refuse, both Mr. Harwood and Stanley will be sent to the work house for thirty days.

This case is closed."

"But your Lordship, they dropped the charges against the defendant in good faith."

"I know that, but they treated Mr. Nibs with great disrespect and that is exhibiting bad feelings between the British and our American Visitors. I am punishing them because they showed bad judgment and could have created an international incident and put Great Britain in a bad light with the rest of the world. We could have suffered great financial damage by having foreign visitors boycotting Great Britain over this incident. I am making Harwood and Stanley examples of what will happen to those people that advance disrespect upon out tourist and visitors which could cause a negative affect or disruption of the economical future of England which might lead to the down fall of the British Empire and then we would all be at the mercy of some foreign power take over such as the United States or even Ireland. And if that were to happen and had I not acted when I could have my name would go down in history as the judge that caused the down fall of British Empire and I could possibly be the most hated man in all history. Now really Lord Sniff Snuff would you want me and my descendant to carry that heavy burden for the rest of our lives?

"No your Lordship I would not. I withdraw my protest."

"Nibs thanks your Lordship for his generous verdict and says anytime you have a vacation coming up, he'll send his private jet to pick you and your family up and take you anywhere you want to go."

"Mr. Nibs is quite welcome, and I shall take him up on his kind and generous offer. Perhaps Mr. Nibs can help me in choosing the right stocks to invest in?"

"Nibs said invest in his newest stock and you will be able to retire a rich man in only one year."

"Really, old chap? By Jove then I'll do that. Which stock might that be?

"Nibs said gold dust kitty litter. It is made of real gold dust for the rich fat cats and the stock is at forty points and rising daily."

"By Jove I'll get to it right after court. And thank you Mr. Nibs."

Nibs, Mr. Cuttleworth, Mr. Wilson, Bentley, O'Harrah, Howard, Tracy and Marcia are all sitting around in Nibs' hotel suite once again. "After Mr. Harwood heard Mr. Nibs' testimony he sure turned tail and dropped his complaint against me." O'Harrah remarks.

"It was also very nice of the judge to force Mr. Harwood to give us the red carpet treatment and to eat in his restaurant for free even though Nibs could well afford to pay for it."

"We could have turned around and sued the pants off Mr. Harwood for false arrest and harassment if we had wanted to, but Mr. Nibs said to let it go." Wilson says.

"The lobsters were so good too and Mr. Harwood was so nice to be our private waiter." Bentley says.

"Stanley helped too did you see how he jumped every time we asked for something?" Howard quizzes.

"He knew if he hadn't jumped, Judge Winston would have jumped on him instead." Marcia says.

"All of this excitement has been very stressful for poor Mr. Nibs, the dear old soul." Tracy says with concern.

"I must say that was the best service I ever received in any restaurant in my life and the wine was superb." O'Harrah remarks.

"Nibs said the fish steaks were the best he had ever eaten and the oyster stew was perfect.'

"Boy old Harwood was sure scraping and bowing to Mr. Nibs and calling him sir and all." Howard quips.

"If he had treated Master Nibs that way in the beginning the judge wouldn't have told him off in court and made him serve Master Nibs and all his employees' free meals." Bentley injects.

"That must have come to you as a great surprise, O'Harrah, to find out you and Judge Winston were cousins?" Cuttleworth quizzes.

"Yes it most certainly was and as we were leaving his court room he invited me to visit him at his manor house outside of London sometime for tea and crumpets."

"What's a crumpet?" asks Marcia.

"It's a crumbled up cookie." Howard quips.

"These English have a word for everything I believe a crumpet is a tasteless English cracker." Wilson suggests.

"Nibs said he believes it's a kind of dog biscuit made for humans."

"Well I'd be very careful if I was you O'Harrah, you never know what might be in one of those crumpets, and you might even come down with some rare foreign illness from eating a crumpet." Tracy warns.

"Then you could sue your cousins the judge and end up owning his manor house." Wilson says.

"Now I really don't believe my cousin would serve me something that would make me ill."

"If your cousin can well afford a manor house then he can certainly afford to serve you something better than a stale cracker." Cuttleworth remarks.

"The English seem pretty stale themselves at times." says Howard.

"If Master Nibs hadn't been so tired from his long day in court and his horrible night in the pound; I am sure he would have gone to see the London version of the play, Cats" Bentley says with a sigh.

"Nibs said he plans on seeing that play this evening after he has dinner with the queen."

"Really, Mr. Nibs has been invited to have dinner with the queen?" asks Marcia.

"Well not exactly, but I'm hoping we can arrange for the queen to invite him for dinner at Buckingham Palace this afternoon."

"That would certainly put a light back into Master Nibs life after that horrible ordeal that he suffered at the hands of that nasty Mr. Harwood." Bentley remarks.

"I still feel good about punching that low life in the nose for insulting Mr. Nibs by calling him a filthy animal."

"It looks like old Harwood was the filthy animal." Howard says with a chuckle.

"So where else does Mr. Nibs plan to go today?" Marcia asks.

"Nibs said he wants to see London Bridge, the Tower of London, Piccadilly Circus, and the Common."

"I thought they moved London Bridge to Arizona?" Bentley quizzes.

"Why did they do that?" asks Howard.

"Because London Bridge was falling down and they didn't want it to fall on some of those snobby Londoners, so they sold it to the Arizonans." Wilson replies.

"So they sold it to the Arizonans so it would fall on them, huh?" Cuttleworth asks.

"You mean the circus is still in town after all of this time?" Howard asks.

"My cousin the judge probably asked them to stay another day so Mr. Nibs could see the circus."

"Why on earth would Mr. Nibs want to go see common people in London after coming all of this way from America?" Marcia asks.

"Well if he can't see London Bridge, then maybe he'll buy London Bridge from the Arizonans and move it to his winter house." Cuttleworth says.

"Isn't his winter home in Arizona?" Bentley asks.

"That's right it is, then Nibs can just look out his rear windows and see London Bridge from there."

"Is London Bridge near his winter home?" Marcia asks.

"Well it's in Arizona and Nibs' winter home is in Arizona."

"Arizona is a big state and it could be anywhere in it." Wilson explains.

"Nibs winter house is a big house and covers a lot of ground, so he is bound to see it from one of his windows."

"Mr. Nibs should be careful when he is at Piccadilly Circus with all of those people crowded in under the tent. I have heard those big tents can get pretty hot inside and I would hate to se Mr. Nibs come down with heat exhaustion." Tracy warns.

"How high is the Tower of London?" asks Howard.

"I think it might be a little higher than the Empire State Building in New York City.

I think the Tower of London is the highest building in the world."

Wilson suggests.

"My word, what is it used for?" Bentley asks in astonishment.

"It's an office building built right after World War Two because they needed more office space so the Lords and Ladies could conduct business and there wasn't much room on the ground with London growing so big." Wilson tries to explain.

"My word, I never realized those Londoners had the intelligence to build anything that high." Cuttleworth whistles.

"One other reason they had to build it so high was to be able to see above the London fog, otherwise they wouldn't be able to know whether or not if the world ever came to an end." Wilson explains.

"Surely they would know whether the world came to an end or not because it would end for them too." O'Harrah says with doubt in his words.

"Not necessarily with so much pea soup fog surrounding them, they would just think the pea soup was getting thicker and hotter." replies Wilson.

"While Master Nibs is here he ought to see the church where the Queens are crowned." Bentley suggests.

"You mean to say kings actually batter their wives?" Howard quizzes.

"What Bentley means is the queens are coroneted, Bentley didn't mean they were crowned by a weapon." O'Harrah explains.

"What does coroneted mean?" Howard asks.

"Haven't you ever heard of coroneted milk?" Marcia asks.

"That's Carnation Milk." O'Harrah explains.

"So what happens to them, do the kings pour milk over their heads?" Howard asks.

"I'd like to pour something over your head and I didn't have milk in mind either. I was thinking more on the lines of cement after placing you in a barrel." Wilson quips.

"Now, now; we are all here to enjoy a vacation with Nibs, so let's not start threatening anyone." Cuttleworth cautions.

"You can hardly say we are enjoying a vacation with Howard hanging around." O'Harrah injects.

"Nibs said he needs Howard to drive him."

"What to drive him crazy?" Wilson asks.

"Mr. Nibs should also go and see the wax museum and to be sure to see Big Ben while he is here, he shouldn't miss Big Ben." O'Harrah suggests.

"I don't believe Nibs wants to meet any more Londoners, he didn't come all this way to meet some giant."

"I believe Big Ben is a clock." Wilson explains.

"Now why on earth would Nibs want to go see a clock when he has lots of clocks of his own? In fact he inherited an abandon clock store in Corona, New Mexico full of old clocks. In fact there is suppose to be enough clocks in that old abandon building to give everyone in the state of New Mexico a free clock. Why he might even open up a clock museum in the town of Corona."

"This isn't just any clock it's the world's largest clock." O'Harrah says.

"So what, a clock is a clock. Whether it's a big clock or a small clock, they al tell the same time."

"But this clock is on a high tower of the Parliament Building where the English make their laws." Wilson says.

"Oh, so that's where they made that stupid law barring Nibs from eating in that restaurant, is it?"

"O'Harrah ought to go down there and punch them all in the nose for passing that law on Mr. Nibs." Howard says.

"No, no, they weren't the ones to pass that law they only make national laws affecting all of Great Britain." Wilson explains.

"Nibs isn't interested in seeing a building where they make laws and have to have a big clock to tell time. Why can't they just buy glasses like everybody else if they have to make the clock that big just to see it?"

"Dear me, it seems these Londoners all have bad eye sight to have to make that clock so large for everyone to see it?" Tracy says with a sigh.

"It's probably all of that thick pea soup fog that causes their failing eye sight." Howard suggests.

"At least no one in London will every go hungry as long as they have pea soup for fog." Marcia injects.

"Mr. Wilson, I want you to call the queen and have her invite Nibs over for dinner at Buckingham Palace. Then I want you to reserve seats for eight including Nibs at Piccadilly Circus, and make sure they are front row seats right up next to the ring.

Then I want everybody to leave except Bentley, Nibs needs his rest before going out this afternoon to have dinner with the queen and see the sights."

CHAPTER THREE

BACK HOME IN INDIANA

Nibs, Mr. Cuttleworth, Mr. Wilson, Bentley, O'Harrah, Howard, Tracy and Marcia are all aboard Nibs' yacht the Cat Fish at sea on their way back to America after spending several days in London.

"It's good to be on our way back home again. Nibs is still pretty upset that the Queen refused to invite him to Buckingham Palace for dinner. He just can't understand why the queen was allergic to cats."

"I tried explaining to her that he was no ordinary cat, but a wealthy American real estate tycoon cat, but she just seemed not to care." Wilson says.

"Maybe she misunderstood you and thought you said he was a raccoon instead of a tycoon." O'Harrah suggests.

"Poor Master Nibs was so disappointed in not being able to have dinner with the queen his heart was so set on it." Bentley says with a sigh.

"There wasn't any circus either, those Londoners have been misleading American into believing there was a circus in town so people would come all the way to London to see it and then be disappointed. That's fraud!" Howard exclaims irritated.

"Yes, it was just some old cross streets with a bunch of people driving on the wrong side of the road." Marcia adds.

"The Tower of London was the biggest disappointment of all.

It was just a big old ugly castle with towers where they had a bunch of fancy jewels and no fancy cat collars either." says Cuttleworth.

"I think Mr. Nibs was pretty bored with the whole thing as he seemed to sleep a lot in the back of the limousine." Wilson says.

"I can't understand why those London police officers pulled me over claiming I was driving on the wrong side of the road; I wasn't driving on the wrong side of the road, those Londoners were." Howard says.

"If Mr. Nibs hadn't told you to stop arguing with those police officers we would have all been thrown in jail again and ended up in another court and Mr. Nibs more then likely would have been taken to the pound again." Wilson says.

"That would have surely caused Mr. Nibs to have a complete nervous break down." Tracy says with concern.

"Nibs said he wished he had never gone to London. That he never got to meet Puss in Boots or the queen, yet Puss in Boots was able to see the queen in London Towne."

"Puss in Boots was a fairy tale." Wilson explains.

"I thought Puss in Boots was a cat?" Howard quizzes.

"Yeah, I thought Puss in Boots was a cat too?" adds Marcia.

"I never knew fairies had tails, but then I never knew judges in London wore women's wigs either, so maybe English fairies do have tails." O'Harrah quips trying to get Wilson's goat.

"Look the fairies didn't have tails, the fairies were in tales." Wilson tries very hard to explain.

"So were they wearing tuxedos with tails?" asks Howard

"How strange, why were the fairies in tails?" Marcia asks.

"Most likely so they could cast a spell while wagging their tails." Howard suggests.

"Were they cat tails or dog tails?" O'Harrah asks now holding back a chuckle.

"No, they were not those kinds of tails, they were stories." Wilson explains, his face turning red with frustration.

"So now you're telling us you just made up a story so Mr. Nibs wouldn't feel sorry for not meeting Puss in Boots who got to see the queen, which he didn't. Well what was so special about Puss in Boots that she got to see the queen?" Howard asks.

"I know both Puss in boots and the queen were ladies so naturally the queen would see a strange lady cat before she would meet with a strange man cat." Marcia says trying to be helpful.

"Look all of you! Puss in Boots was only in a Mother Goose story and there never was a real Puss in Boots!" exclaims Wilson now raising his voice in anger.

"So now you are trying to tell us that some mother goose lied to you and told you that there was never any Puss in Boots in order that wouldn't make Mr. Nibs feel bad that he didn't get to meet this pussy cat which actually met with the queen." Howard says.

"Why Mr. Wilson, I didn't know you could talk with geese, how come you didn't tell be you could talk to a goose? I would have had Nibs invite her to spend the weekend at his city apartment home."

"I never said I could talk to a goose. Mother Goose was the pen name of the author who wrote children's nursery rhyme, she wasn't a goose."

"If she wasn't a goose why was she kept in a pen then?"

"Probably so Puss in Boots couldn't eat her for dinner." Howard suggests.

"Cooked goose does sound rather appetizing." Bentley says smacking his lips.

"Sounds like Mr. Wilson's goose is cooked because of his lying to Mr. Nibs about Puss in Boots." O'Harrah says with a chuckle.

"Nibs said he doesn't want to hear anymore about Puss in Boots, the queen, London or anything else."

"Oh poor Mr. Nibs is becoming stressed out from all of his bad experiences of the last few days." Tracy says showing concern.

"All in all we did get to see the beefeaters at Buckingham Palace do the changing of the guard." Marcia says.

"How do you know they were beef eaters; they might have been fish eaters for all you know?" Howard says.

"Fish is much better for you than beef." Tracy adds.

"Yeah Marcia, how do you know the guards ate beef, did you ask them?" O'Harrah quips in fun.

"That's just what they called, beefeaters." Marcia answers.

"Well they didn't look like beef eaters to me, they looked more like vegetarians." Wilson quips now getting in on the fun.

"Nibs said they looked more like toy soldiers with over sized dog fur caps on their heads."

"Did you see that big department store named after me?" O'Harrah asks.

"Where do you come up with that it was named after you?

Why as I remember it, it was spelled different." Wilson says.

"I remember that place, but it wasn't spelled d-i-f-f-e-r-e-n-t at all, but more like h-a-r-r-o-d-s." Marcia says.

"I told you if you hung out with Howard too long you'd be talking just like him." Wilson says to Marcia.

"Nibs wants to turn in for the night. We'll be back in the states in a few days and Nibs wants to get all the rest he can from his exhausting

London trip."

◇◇◇◇◇◇◇

Nibs, Mr.Cuttleworth, Bentley, Mr. Wilson, O'Harrah, Howard, Tracy, and Marcia are all back in Nibs' apartment back in America.

"Nibs said he is so very happy to be back home again in Indiana and away from that terrible place called London."

"Where they have talking geese and cats running around wearing boots." Howard jests.

"Howard, you've not a bit funny, in fact you're down right boring and Mr. Nibs should have left you in London with all of the other crazies." Wilson says.

"Then how come you didn't stay?" Howard quizzes Wilson.

"I don't know why everybody picks on Howard all the time?

The rest of you make remarks and jokes just as often as Howard does." Marcia says in defense of Howard.

"The dear girl is right don't throw stones at bad acting clowns if you're a bad acting clown yourself." Bentley says.

"That's don't throw stones at glass houses." O'Harrah corrects.

"Yes, especially if there are people inside them, someone could get hurt from broken glass." Tracy adds.

"Nibs said next time he will go to Paris."

"Ah Paris in the springtime, Paris in the fall, I love Paris in all." sings Wilson.

"So you saw that movie back in the fifties too where that French girl sang to that aging Hollywood actor." O'Harrah reminiscences .

"She was called Gigi." Wilson says.

"Well gee---gee you don't say." Howard quips.

"I'd love to go to Paris I'll bet they wouldn't treat Mr. Nibs like those Londoners did." Marcia adds.

"The French I heard love cats. They call their women pussy cat and the word meow is French." Howard quips.

"I didn't know that?" Cuttleworth quizzes in wonderment.

"Me-ow a French word, where on earth did you hear that? Me-ow is the sound a cat makes it's not a French word." Wilson tells Howard.

"Oh yeah, I guess you never have been to the Paris alleys at night, they say there are dozens of alley cats roaming about me-owing." Howard replies.

"I hope when Mr. Nibs goes to Paris he doesn't bring Howard with him." Wilson says.

"Do you think they'll have French fries and Frenched head lights in Paris?" Marcia asks.

"Oh I hope Mr. Nibs doesn't eat too may French Fries, they are so greasy and it would be bad for on Mr. Nibs health." Tracy says with concern.

"There's a lot more to see in Paris than in London, the Louvre, and Notre Dame, the Arch of Triumph, the Eiffel Tower and the beautiful women." Wilson says.

"Why do the call it the Eiffel Tower?" asks Marcia.

"More than likely it's because when you go up in it you get a real eyeful of the city." Howard suggests.

"Ah the Louvre, that's what I want to see." Bentley says drawing in his breath.

"You want to go all the way to Paris just to get a lube job? Heck Joe's garage up the street can give you a good lube job without going all of the way to Paris." Howard remarks.

"Bentley said Louvre, not lube." Wilson corrects.

"There for a minute I thought he was trying to talk like one of those stuffy Englishmen." Howard quips.

"What's a Louvre?" Marcia asks.

"A French lube job." Howard quips.

"The Louvre is a museum in Paris where the finest art work in the world is there.

The Mona Lisa is there." Wilson explains.

"How do you know she is still there? Do you think she is still waiting for you after you stood up her years ago?" Howard quips.

"Nibs said he can't wait to see gay Purée."

"Is she a cat like Puss in boots who lives in Paris?" Howard asks.

"Howard, where did you get your education? In a Cracker Jack box?" asks Wilson.

"I finished high school."

"What, after eight years of flunking the first year?" O'Harrah asks holding back a laugh.

"I don't believe he has ever gone to school. Why if he tried they would probably would have expelled him permanently as a danger to the further education of morons." Wilson quips.

"Nibs said he might even go to the French Riviera or India instead."

"I'd rather go to India myself." injects Howard.

"Maybe if you ask nicely Mr. Nibs will send you there on a one way ticket by yourself." Wilson quips.

"Do you think Mr. Nibs would send me too?" asks Marcia.

"Why not? That way we get two birds with one stone." Wilson says holding back a chuckle.

"It sounds alright to me." O'Harrah chuckles.

"Master Nibs I am sure would love two birds." Bentley remarks.

"Why not make it three birds and send Bentley along to keep them company?" Wilson quizzes.

"Nibs said he is thinking about getting a new attorney, one that doesn't insults his employees. He is also thinking about getting a much better and serious chauffeur.

One that he can depend on and doesn't make jokes every time some one opens their mouth, a smarter secretary, a nicer body guard and a more intelligent valet."

"Is he thinking about getting a new nurse too?" Tracy asks.

"No, not as long as you don't act like the rest of his employees."

"But I have even gone to jail for protecting Mr. Nibs." pleads O'Harrah.

"Exactly! That and your insults are going to be your down fall."

"Aren't I a good driver?" asks Howard.

"Yes, but you talk too much, joke too much, and make snipe remarks to everyone.

I even heard you whispering jokes to Marcia during our London trial."

"Is there something wrong with my secretarial work?" asks Marcia. "No, that's fine. It's your dumb blond attitude that Nibs doesn't like."

"But I'm actually a brunette. I bleached my hair blond."

"Oh? Well then why don't you act like a brunette instead of a dumb blond?"

"I thought I was an excellent valet." Bentley quizzes.

"That you are, but you're also a big bore."

"Haven't I always been a good attorney for Mr. Nibs and his employees." asks Wilson.

"Nibs never said you weren't, but you are much too insulting to his employees."

"If Mr. Nibs let most of his employees go he would get very depressed realizing the great mistake he made then he would become even more depressed because he would miss the very character of everyone. Why if Mr. Nibs got rid of O'Harrah he wouldn't get to hear anymore Scottish jokes. If he got rid of Marcia he would not have her around to make him laugh. If he lost Howard Marcia would not be able defend Howard, when Bentley wasn't around there wouldn't be anyone to address him as Master Nibs, and when he was rid of Mr. Wilson he wouldn't hear anyone taking jabs at everyone else including his enemies." Tracy reports.

"Nibs said that is the most you have said since you have been in his employment.

He didn't know you were so bright, caring about others, and pleading for their jobs.

Nibs said you'd make a better attorney than Mr. Wilson, but he'll keep Wilson.

He said since you were willing to speak for the others as you did, he won't fire anybody after all."

No one says anything. The silence is deafening! A clock can be heard ticking on the wall of Nibs' living room. A tick-tick-tick-tick sound is the only sound to be heard for nearly three minutes as everyone in the room just sits looking straight ahead with their hands folded together, sitting without moving, and with blank expressionless faces.

"Nibs said he can't stand it any longer; he wants everybody back like they were and wants no one to change."

"Now since that is over, I'd like a raise." says O'Harrah.

"Nibs said if you want a raise take the elevator to the top floor."

"I would like a day off." Bentley injects.

"Nibs said you're always slightly off and usually more than a day."

"Since everybody is asking for something, I'd like more money." says Howard.

"Nibs said you should marry a girl with money."

"I'd like a computer to help me with my secretarial work." Marcia adds.

"Nibs said he knows where you can make easy monthly payments on one with only a hundred dollars down."

"I'm in need of an assistant." Wilson says.

"Nibs said get yourself a dog from the pound."

"I don't want anything." Tracy says.

"Don't worry Nibs said he hadn't planned on giving you anything either."

"How come Mr. Nibs is such a tight wad with his employees, yet he buys a whole building and allows homeless people to live in it for free?" O'Harrah asks.

"Nibs said if you still want him to fire you he will, then you'll be homeless too and you can live in that building for free too."

"Aren't we ever going to get a raise?" Howard asks.

"Nibs said you are free to go up in elevators any time you like."

"It seems Mr. Nibs is starting to act more like his employees." Wilson quips.

"He's had good teachers."

"Really, who were they?" Marcia asks.

"Really and truly, you ought to know you were one of them."

"Who are the others?" asks Howard.

"Do you work for Nibs?"

"As little as possible."

"He's what you might call a part-time teacher." Wilson quips.

"Then Mr. Wilson must be the principal because his mouth is nearly always working over time" Bentley quips.

"Nibs, ah! Things are back to normal once more."

CHAPTER FOUR

PEACE AH PEACE

It is one week later in the apartment of Nibs and Mr. Cuttleworth in the old tenement building that is now completely remodeled. In fact their apartment has been enlarged and the floors are covered in rich red carpeting. The walls have been paneled in dark rich mahogany. There are crystal and highly polished brass chandeliers overhead.

The furniture is all done in dark mahogany and red velvet. More windows have been added and red velvet drapes with gold colored fringe and cords hold them back from new lead window frames.

A large television console and stereo cabinet is at one end of the now very large living room. Gold gilded framed oil paintings hang from the walls. Tiffany lamps set on tables and as floor lamps. Expensive French and Italian vases and pots set about on ornate mahogany shelves. The classics line glass covered book cases. Rare antiques set on low shelves and even on the floor.

Marble statues of lions and cats adorn the empty spaces against the walls. A very fancy ornate solid mahogany door with a peep hole leads to the hall. An arched entrance way leads to the now massive dining room with its expensive china and crystal ware. There are highly ornate mahogany armchairs surrounding the table and a large red and gold Persian rug covers the floor.

A fine three tiered crystal and gold chandelier hangs directly above the dining room table. It is afternoon. Mr. Cuttleworth is lounging in a fine red velvet covered armchair.

Nibs is washing himself on an antique armless chair next to Mr. Cuttleworth. Mr. Wilson and O'Harrah are sitting on a fine mahogany and red velvet Victorian couch. Marcia and Tracy are sitting in wing chairs nearby. Howard and Bentley are sitting on a loveseat across the room. A large grandfather clock ticks, ticks in one corner.

"I have gathered you all together this afternoon to discuss our former trip to London and what Nibs plans on doing in the near future." says Cuttleworth to those sitting in the room.

"I would think Mr. Nibs wanted to put his London trip behind him?" Wilson says.

"Golly Mr. Nibs must think he has a large behind to think he can put our entire London trip behind himself." Howard jokes.

"Howard! That remark was uncalled for!" exclaims Wilson.

"Nibs said he was very disappointed in his trip to London. That everything he heard in the travel folders wasn't true and he was lead to believe things would be different.

He says since he paid so much for the Cat Fish that he wants to get more service out of it and plans on taking a long ocean voyage this time."

"I didn't know Mr. Nibs ordered cat fish? Was that at old Harwood's fancy restaurant or where?" Marcia asks.

"Marcia, you've getting as stupid as Howard. The Cat Fish is Mr. Nibs' yacht we went to London in. Don't you remember?" O'Harrah asks.

"Oh, I didn't know the name of the yacht. I thought it didn't have a name."

"Everybody names their yachts. It's been an old custom the world over." Wilson explains.

"Oh I do hope Mr. Nibs won't become ill from a long sea voyage." Tracy says.

"Where does the master plan on going?" Bentley asks.

"Nibs said he is thinking of going in to the Pacific by the way of the Panama Canal."

"Pana Ma's canal? I didn't know Pana Ma had a canal. Did Pana Pa dig it for her?" quips Howard.

"Howard are you just stupid or you making a joke?" O'Harrah asks disgusted.

"Howard is a joke." Wilson replies.

"The Panama Canal was built in the teens of the last century.

It was built by Americans." Cuttleworth tells Howard.

"Teens were responsible for building the Panama Canal?" asks Marcia puzzled.

"No, it was built some time between nineteen ten and nineteen, nineteen," replies Cuttleworth.

"So you did not have to repeat it Mr. Cuttleworth, I heard the nineteen the first time," Marcia replies.

"I was not repeating the year that was merely the year that ended the teens of the twentieth century in which the Panama Canal had been built."

"Were they American mothers?" asks Marcia.

"Why would you ask that?" Wilson asks Marcia.

"Mr. Cuttleworth said they were maws, so I would assume they were American maws since he said Americans built it."

"I believe the lady was affected by the London fog." injects Bentley.

"The so-called-lady was affected by a moron the day she was born." O'Harrah says.

"How do you know, O'Harrah? Were you there?" asks Marcia.

"And you were affected by a donkey the day you were born.

He ran off with your brains." Everyone except O'Harrah burst out laughing, even Nibs rolls over and meows happily.

"Nibs said that was the funniest joke he ever heard from Marcia."

"But then Marcia must have been the donkey." Quips O'Harrah.

"So I suppose you were there?" quizzes Howard.

"One didn't need to be there when she was born to figure that out." explains O'Harrah.

"Nibs said he would like to get as far away from London as possible. It was a bad experience all around. He said he just wants to find peace and quiet away from the maddening crowd."

"Yeah away from Howard and Marcia. They are the king and queen of the maddening crowd." O'Harrah quips.

"Nibs plans on having everyone go with him."

"Maybe he can put up with them, but what about the rest of us?" asks Wilson.

"Oh the rest of you will surely drive poor Mr. Nibs mad." Marcia quips.

"You have nerve to talk Marcia. It is you and that idiot of a chauffeur that drives Nibs mad." O'Harrah remarks.

"Nibs said he just thought everyone acts natural since that is the way he has always seen humans act. Why Mrs. Burnside and Sarah Felts acted strange too by cat standards.

But Nibs says he has come to believe that all humans act this way naturally."

"Perhaps the Londoners have rubbed off on everyone." Bentley suggests.

"I am starting to believe the Londoners were sane compared to Howard and Marcia." O'Harrah remarks.

"The experience was enough to drive any one mad." says Tracy.

"Come to think of it now, Marcia seems to have changed drastically since our London trip." Wilson says.

"Because she had a chance to be in the company of Howard long enough to start to acting like him." says O'Harrah chuckling.

"Nibs said since our London trip was so bad he is glad he did not go to Paris as it might have been far worse."

"And those Londoners are such braggarts. Did you see how big the sign was for that small plain yard the Scotchman had?

And his house was larger than this entire building." Marcia says.

"Can you imagine Mr. Nibs putting up a large sign in front of this building; Nibs' yard?" Howard remarks.

"What yard? That little strip of green between the building and the sidewalk can barely qualify as a yard." Marcia says.

"Well the Scotchman's yard wasn't much bigger." Howard says.

"Nibs said everything about the Londoners was either misleading or out right bragging of something they didn't have, like Piccadilly Circus. Why they didn't even have elephants or tigers."

"But they sure had plenty of clowns and monkeys with the way they drove their cars." O'Harrah quips.

"Dear me, and London Bridge was the biggest disappointment of all." sighs Bentley.

"London Bridge? They didn't have London Bridge. It had been moved to Arizona years before." Wilson explains.

"Yes Sir, but that is why it was such a big disappointment." replies Bentley.

"I don't remember seeing any pea soup fog while we were there." Tracy injects.

"Mr. Nibs paid off the weatherman to keep it away while he was there." Wilson quips.

"Really, I thought it was a natural phenomenon?" quizzes Tracy.

"What's a natural phenomenon?" asks Howard.

"Oh I know that one. It's a pneumonia you get when you go to a strange country like London." Marcia replies.

"A pneumonia Marcia? A strange phenomenon is you existing." O'Harrah says sarcastically.

"And don't forget Howard." Wilson adds.

"And don't forget Puss in Boots," Marcia remarks.

94

"Yes, Puss in Boots went to London when it was a town to see the queen, but she didn't allow typhoons in the palace, so Puss in Boots blew out of there to see Mother Goose about a dozen golden eggs, but she was out of golden eggs , so she went to Nursery Rhyme where she bought a dozen silver eggs because they were no longer on the gold standard, but Nursery Rhyme was only selling black market eggs, so she ended up buying a dozen white eggs in the middle of the night because the black market only opened between sun down and sun up on accord it was a black market."

"Howard, no one wants to hear your account of Puss in Boots," Wilson sighs shaking his head side to side.

"Yeah on account Howard is crazy." O'Harrah remarks.

"And dear me but there was little to really see in London." Bentley says.

"I liked Buckingham Palace and the Tower of London." Marcia says.

"Why do they call it Buckingham Palace?" Howard asks.

"Because when you and Marcia showed up they didn't want any hams around so they bucked the two of you out of the palace," Wilson explains with a chuckle.

"What about that big clock up on that tower that went bong, bong all of the time?" Howard asks.

"Nibs said it didn't have to be so loud. Why anyone could look up there and see what time it was without all that noise."

"When it found out Howard and Marcia was in town it bonged, bonged to warn the Londoners." quips O'Harrah.

"However it could have been warning us of Londoners." Wilson quips back.

"And that awful noise of the clock and the strange wailing like sirens of their police cars was enough to drive some one mad." Tracy says.

"But it was nothing compared to Howard and Marcia." O'Harrah says.

"But you and Mr. Wilson are worse." Marcia says.

"You think they were bad. You should have met Mrs. Burnside. Why she had a one track mind. The only thing on her mind was the rent. That's all she ever cared about; the rent this, the rent that. She never cared rather or not Nibs or I were ill or under the weather. All she could think of is when I was going to pay the rent? Rent, rent, rent. Why I believe that was the only important word in the English language she seemed to know."

"Sort of like Honey Pott Wypout. All she had on her mind was money." Wilson says.

"Oh but she was a terrible person and so greedy." Cuttleworth says.

"So how does she get by now that she used up all the money her husband left to her?" O'Harrah asks.

"Last time I heard she was going steady with a wealthy undertaker by the name of Barry M. Deep." Cuttleworth replies.

"Barry M. Deep? I know him. He was once my client. If she thinks for one minute that old Deep is going to fork over any of his money to her, she has another think coming. Why Barry is so tight with his money you couldn't pry it loose from him with a wrecking bar. I took a case for him and won, but when it came to getting my fee he held out so long that I had to start proceedings to sue him. And then when he finally came around to paying me with the threat of being sued, he hemmed and hawed about the fee, wasting two hours of my time." Wilson says.

"Perhaps it was you ridiculously high fees that he was squabbling over? I well remember how you kept adding on charges for simple little things like a blank check and secretarial services when you had no secretary."

"Those were just standard procedures like you would pay anyone." Wilson explains.

"Nibs said that is baloney. You were shystering me."

"I had to make a living."

"Who, from the dying?" Cuttleworth asks in disgust.

"When is Mr. Nibs planning on going on his next trip?" asks Tracy.

"Soon, soon, but first he says he needs to plan his route. He says he wants to go island hoping around the Pacific."

"Oh that is silly. A cat can't hop like a rabbit. And anyway no rabbit can leap that high from island to island." Marcia says.

"What Mr. Nibs had in mind was to go from one island to the other." O'Harrah explains.

"What other?" Howard quizzes.

"He was thinking perhaps Easter Island, Pitcairn and Fiji."

"Who did you want to feed Howard?" asks Marcia.

"He is old enough to feed himself." Cuttleworth answers.

"Then why on earth did you tell Howard you wanted to get some one to feed him?" asks Marcia.

"Mr. Nibs said Fiji, not feed him. Fiji is an island in the South

Pacific." O'Harrah explains to Marcia.

"Nibs said he wants everyone to go out and buy clothes for the South Pacific."

"Well I'm not going to buy any clothes for the South Pacific. Let the South Pacific buy its own clothes." says Marcia.

"The South Pacific is an ocean, Stupid." O'Harrah says.

"I don't care if it is an ocean stupid, I am still not buying any clothes for it."

"What Nibs means is everyone ought to buy themselves a new wardrobe for warm balmy weather."

"Whose balmy or whether?" Howard quips.

"You are my boy, you are." Wilson answers as a matter of fact.

"I have been to the South Pacific, but I never was in to clothing of the climate. I'd rather wear what I wear now." Bentley says.

"Everyday, won't they get dirty wearing them every day?" Marcia quizzes.

"Not these same clothes, but ones like them. Rather strange questions, Marcia."

"Why bother explaining anything to her, Bentley? You've just wasting your energy." O'Harrah says.

"Nibs said he has to get the London trip off of his mind. It was a real nightmare.

He wants a fully relaxing ocean voyage and to lay on tropical island beaches eating exotic mice and lapping up exotic milk to try and forget London."

"What about Puss in Boots?" Howard asks.

"What about Puss in Boots?" Cuttleworth asks.

"Does he want to forget her too?"

"Nibs said he doesn't know her and doesn't want to know her if she is anything like the rest of the Londoners."

"But Puss in Boots is in London visiting the queen." Says Marcia matter factly.

"But I thought Puss in Boots was turned away because she would not bring the queen any golden eggs laid by the goose from Nursery Rhyme?"

"No Howard, she turned Puss in Boots away because she bought her eggs on the black market and the queen won't do business with shady deals."

"Shady deals? You can hardly call buying eggs at night shady deals." Howard replies.

"Hey you two, quit talking about Puss in Boots. Besides you have it all turned around.

Nibs said Mr. Wilson is a historian and an authority on Puss in Boots and if you want to know anything about Puss in Boots you need to get educated by Mr. Wilson."

Cuttleworth tells Howard and Marcia.

"But Sir, I know next to nothing when it comes to Puss in Boots. In fact I only got my education on it in kindergarten." Explains Wilson.

"Oh so that explains why you are such a lousy attorney if you only went to kindergarten,"

Cuttleworth quips as everyone except Wilson bursts out laughing.

"How long before we actually leave to go to the Cat Fish?" Wilson asks.

"Nibs said in six days. So everyone prepare to go where everything is trouble free at last."

"Trouble free? Taking Mr. Nibs' servants with him everywhere can hardly be considered trouble free Mr. Cuttleworth," Tracy remarks.

"But Nibs said he must have his servants to be trouble free in case he has any problems."

"Having his servants seems to be his biggest problems already," Tracy replies.

"What would you say if you were on an un-chartered island all by your self and all your servants were mice and birds, Nibs?" asked Cuttleworth.

"Peace ah peace at last." Nibs replies.

THE END